THE BITTERSWEET MISADVENTURES BOOK 1

My Own Little Tin Box

The Bittersweet Misadventures, Book 1:
My Own Little Tin Box

Copyright © 2016 by Cata Muñoz

ISBN-13: 978-0-9966531-6-9

Book Design by Logotecture

First Edition

Printed in the U.S.A.

Writestream Publishing, LLC
Parker Ford, PA
writestreampublishing.com

THE BITTERSWEET MISADVENTURES BOOK 1

My Own Little Tin Box

CATA MUÑOZ

Dedicated to

Pul (the greatest) and charles

0

The small shop in front of our school sold the best homemade pretzels I had ever tasted; perfectly crunchy, and with the perfect amount of salt crystals covering them. Every morning before the school bell rang, we walked into class hungry after having smelled the delicious aroma of what we called "pretzel fumes" that came out of the small shop's brick chimney. My mom loved those pretzels, so sometimes while my twin brothers and my father left to play golf on the weekends, we would walk together, and she would buy a big bag of them just for the two of us for breakfast.

Living in a small town like ours had its perks; everything was nearby, and transportation wasn't a problem at all because we walked or rode our bikes and scooters everywhere. It usually rained at night and any other time really, so walking to school in the morning meant getting your rain boots muddy and having a laugh with your friends when you got to class. Everyone was always happy and willing to help out. We lived a simple and entertaining lifestyle with kind neighbors and funny little everyday adventures.

My twin brothers and I have many friends in common, so we go out together most of the time. But right now they had left for a trip with their class to Nice. Ever since they went when they had just turned 15, they had both always wanted to return to France. But I mean, who wouldn't want to, right?

I miss them so much; sometimes I even fall asleep on either of their beds instead of mine, which I'm sure they wouldn't mind at all if they knew; they would surely find their room much more organized when they came back. With them, some of my friends who are in their class went as well, but I always had my two best friends Edric and Victoria.

Victoria is a little shorter than I am. She usually has long black curly hair, but she cut it to shoulder length recently to "make a change" as she calls it. She is so slim that sometimes I ask myself how someone can eat so much and not weigh one single extra pound. Victoria has pale skin and green eyes; she is always by my side. I know I can always count on her, not to mention she is my neighbor. Every time I'm feeling down (which does not happen very often, to be honest), she leaves whatever she's doing and brings in some cookie dough ice cream and strawberries which are my absolute favorite.

Edric, on the other hand, is really tall. He is even taller than I am! Edric has shiny hazel eyes with a peculiar tiny speck of green on the left side of his left eye. He has black hair that falls like a cascade over his head and above the eyes. He is simply charming since he walks Victoria and me home every day after school and during lunch breaks. Edric knows how to have fun and keep Victoria and me out of trouble. That's one of the many reasons why he is such a wonderful friend.

It was Friday night and Victoria, Edric and I had had a long day at school, which meant there wasn't really anything we wanted to do right after, so we had each gone home. Now at 7:15 pm we were meeting at our favorite destination of them all; the abandoned house on the outskirts of town (very close to my house and their's since we lived in such a small urban community). We always met there when we hadn't yet decided where to go because it was close to all of us and it was "our" abandoned house.

This old house had been our special hiding place ever since I can remember. I've never seen anyone around it and it is I could say the safest place to hide your most precious possession. The house is surrounded by the forest and the pine trees with dried pine seeds decorating their roots and twigs scattered all around. Sometimes, a small ray of sunlight manages to pierce through the thick branches of the trees and illuminates the small front porch of the wooden house. Getting inside the house is not hard at all since once you jump the fence and cross the small front sheet of dirt covering the ground, all you have to do is run to the back of the house and go in through the back window which we always make sure to leave a little bit open.

This house is very antique and old-fashioned; maybe that's the best part of it. I like to think of this house as a treasure we found – a hiding place where we can keep our secrets in.

Now at 7:38 pm, I finally got to the house. I was the last one to get there as usual, so I left my red Vespa next to where my friends had left theirs and hurriedly tied my hair up in a quick messy bun and climbed the fence, jumping on the other side. I saw Victoria and Edric sitting on the porch already munching on a bag of chips and three mochas on a recyclable tray sitting next to Edric.

We hadn't been here in a while, I thought to myself, right before Edric read my thoughts and said it out loud as well. Victoria nodded and smiled. I looked at her and smiled back, giggling and agreeing as well.

0.5

We got to the town center and decided to have some dinner. After that, we could just walk around for a while since after all it was an old antique town. Plus walking around town center on a Friday night meant you got to see many friends and acquaintances at some point. We arrived at Green Foods and ate there. Victoria and Edric weren't very enthusiastic about it, but I liked it.

Green as we called it was a kind of a buffet for students. It was an all-you-can-eat place where students in high school, college, and universities could have a healthy meal. We sat with Howard and Daisy at a large round table unconsciously expecting more people to sit with us which usually did happen. After we had all eaten our food, Edric stood up and came back with a big chocolate chip cookie from the desserts table and some vanilla muffins with egg white frosting decorating their usual naked tops.

"It was the last one," he said, giving me one of his charming half smiles.

He placed it in front of me; he knew how much I liked those

cookies, and how fast they always ran out. Francesca, who had just arrived, bolted out of her seat and ran to the desserts table checking eagerly to see if, by any chance, there were any left, but her sad freckled face confirmed what Edric had just said. After a few more people joined us, and after some cupcakes, all our friends had gone home. Once again it was just Victoria, Edric and me.

We walked down the main avenue admiring the substantial amount of people strolling along the street and the life they brought to the town, which was brighter than the elegant light posts themselves. Then, all of a sudden, someone snatched my hat and Victoria's scarf in a split second. Startled and widely amused, we looked around and saw some boys in rusty bicycles laughing loudly and holding them in the air with malice. Victoria looked really upset instantly, Edric and I knew how much that scarf meant to Victoria since it was the only thing she had left from her grandmother.

Edric was the first one to kick off behind them, Victoria and I followed, but it was a bit useless since they had bikes and we only had our feet. I felt so slow, almost as if I wasn't even moving; but we kept going.

We ran behind the thieves as if there was no tomorrow; around corners, behind buildings, crossing the park with our jackets and loose sweater ends flying around swiftly along with my ponytail, our boots hitting the ground stones evenly.

"They are heading towards Mr. Abdelnour's toffee shop!" screamed Edric back at us, trying to control his panting. The store was right there, and there was a dead end after that so they probably wouldn't get any much further.

We ran around the corner and finally got to the toffee shop and found our things just lying on the floor. Victoria grabbed them eagerly and held her scarf tight around her arms smiling as if she was hugging her loved one once again. I took my woven hat and placing it back on my head, grinned at my friends, and gestured for us to leave.

We were still gasping, expelling out white swirls of air from our dry lips into the cold wind.

"Wait, guys, something's odd about this. We can't just leave now," said Edric.

He was right; why had we just found our things lying there? We started looking around for the boys with the bikes looking for any sign of them, but there was nothing around. In fact, there was no one around. That's when we heard a piece of glass being shattered as if someone was stepping on broken pieces. We rushed down the street cautiously looking around for where the sound came from when we saw a shadow walking inside the jewelry store placed on the far end. That was odd, everything around here closed around 8:00 pm and it was nearly 1:00 am already.

We looked a bit closer through the smog and realized the small glass door on the side of the building had been carefully broken. The shadow had now disappeared, but I couldn't seem to stop that eerie feeling inside me, so I turned around and whispered to my two friends that it would be better if we just left and stayed out of whatever was going on before something else happened. Right at that very second a cold hand was gripping the back of my neck. I froze and waited to hear the criminal's rough voice in my ear. But instead, I heard a very familiar one.

"Mr. Gordon?" I asked squinting my eyes as I felt a bitter taste running up my throat. Edric tugged Mr. Gordon's arm and fell to the ground in a strong movement to set me free. Victoria and I leaned down and tried to help Edric get up, but he did so furiously by himself. I cleaned the bit of blood from his ear with my sleeve, noticing broken glass all around us.

Mr. Gordon's police car was parked behind the dumpster with two rusty bikes sitting in the back seat. He noticed I had spotted his car where he was hiding it and tried to grab my arm harshly, but I pulled it away fast enough and looked at him in disgust while looking for a way to escape, observing how he had cornered us in the dead end.

Gordon gasped and looked at us with eyes filled with bitterness and a smirk filled with hatred. "Here's the thing," he said leaning his strong, tall body towards us.

"The two little rats on the bikes were easy to scare away. I took their bikes like snatching a candy out of a baby's hand. Those cowards won't say a thing; I know that. But you three, little miss babble box right here won't keep her mouth shut will she? I'll have to take you three back to the station and charge you with something like breaking into the jewelry store maybe. That will keep us all out of trouble."

"No one would believe you!" said Victoria, with a surprisingly powerful tone in her voice. Mr. Gordon got even closer holding a large black sack of what seemed to be jewels in one hand and looked at her right in the eyes.

"Who are they going to believe little girl? I was just driving around on my night shift and spotted three mischievous students breaking into a store on a Friday night. But you know what Victoria?" he said after he looked away for a quick second. "Maybe they would believe you. You're right. It could be more useful just to shut you off don't you think?"

The poisoned policeman was reaching down for his gun getting a grip on Victoria's wrist as she screamed for help and twisted her body desperately. Sweat ran down Edric's forehead and not knowing what to do he threw dirt over the thief's face blinding him for a second. Mr. Gordon then shot his gun once, thankfully not hitting any of us.

I looked around rapidly and reached down for a thick piece of glass while all this was going on and with all my strength stabbed Mr. Gordon on his right thigh. Falling to the floor and letting go of Victoria we ran away from there with such adrenaline I thought I would soon fly away. Mascara streamed down Victoria's eyes as she cried while we heard a few more gunshots coming our way and Mr. Gordon cursing, repeatedly suggesting he would find us eventually around town and claim his vengeance.

0.75

The next morning, I woke up and stormed down the stairs to turn on the news and see if there was anything about what had happened yesterday, not being able to process the events easily, but remembering how scary it had all been.

My eyes widened when I saw Mr. Gordon at the crime scene being interviewed by Channel 7, Channel 10 and every other news station we had in town. While listening, I immediately noticed he had lied about how he saw the two boys who rode their bikes breaking into the jeweler's shop, and how he was stabbed by one of them before he could arrest them. He continued with his story on how the boys ran away with the precious stones, pearls, and golden jewelry and in desperation had to abandon their bikes, and that was how he had the two metal vehicles. It was perfect, he had the bikes as evidence, and these boys were known to snatch things away like what had happened to Victoria and me. But I knew they had never done anything that serious.

1

I walked down Bandalyard Park, wondering what life would be like if we hadn't taken the risks that we took during winter break and the following months that lead us to this. Now, my two best friends and I had been forced to do community service every Monday, Tuesday, and Wednesday until Christmas break. The problem wasn't doing community service itself, I liked that, but what our parents thought about us now was different, and the thought of Mr. Gordon being around just gave me the worst of chills; even if none of us had actually seen him after what happened at the jewelry shop. You see, a few nights ago it was Valentine's Day. The sun pierced brightly above the windowsill forming delicate sunset lines across the white walls as dusk started to approach. I was at home with Edric and Victoria. We were watching a film as usual since none of us is really interested in Valentine's Day. Before even starting the second movie, we got hungry and ordered a pizza; our favorite pizza, pepperoni, double cheese, tomato, mushrooms and green peppers.

Soon after ordering, the doorbell rang; it was Chuck Morris.

Edric jumped up, and fist pumped his friend just before they hugged as if they were brothers.

"What's going on chicken legs?" said Chuck. He wrestled him till they both fell to the ground.

"What's up Chuckster? Haven't seen you in a while," replied Edric as he covered his face with his right fist and hit Chuck's left shoulder.

Victoria and I watched the little show they put on every time they saw each other, which usually ended with a bloody nose or a "you-hit-me-too-hard-this-time" excuse.

I had known Chuck since I was a little girl. He had short red hair and pale skin, with uncountable freckles staining his face and cheeks. He was tall with nice toned muscles and green eyes that contrasted with his hair perfectly according to Victoria and me. The contrast in his hair and eyes popped out and made him very colorful in some way. Victoria had always been crazy about him, and I thought he was good looking too, but I looked at him more as part of the family.

Somehow Edric and Chuck's fathers had met at a young age and had worked together as teenagers at the Max Brothers Coal Mine after school every day with my dad too. They had then studied the same major in college leading them to later go on to work together both as cartographers. The three of them had been best friends ever since, although my dad wasn't a cartographer like them; but they sure had always stuck together. It wasn't a typical job I know, but they had been very lucky to be able to stay together like that until last year's incident. Chuck and Edric's fathers both passed away in an accident before they returned from one of their missions. I'm not really sure of what happened; all I know is my dad never spoke about it again. Even after what happened, Chuck still came around sometimes, probably because he was used to it, or maybe he just felt alone. Whatever the reason, even if he had been part of the family for so long, there was always an eerie feeling about everything.

Soon we heard the doorbell again, and we all stood up eagerly. Edric hurried outside with the money to pay for our pizza, a wide smile on his face and a growling stomach. As he walked down the steps, Victoria and I decided to follow him, leaving Chuck behind.

The pizza deliverer was kind of weird; he had a creepy glass eye, a pair of huge red earrings and gray hair filling his head except for the bald spot he had on the very top. Everything about him seemed very strange. To top it off, he wore a frightful frown so deep; it seemed to have been carved out with the sharp Exacto knives we use in the art class. Edric, who can be very childish and can get very immature really easily at times, froze and instantly wiped the smile off of his face after taking a look at him. Wide- eyed, he took the pizza in his hands and taking some steps backward quickly signaled us to get back inside the house. He was so concentrated on every little detail of the pizza deliverer that he dropped the money on the sidewalk without paying and without even noticing it. The man began yelling towards the police car that was passing nearby, thinking we wanted to take advantage of his old bones and steal the warm pizza when all that was actually happening was a misunderstanding.

By that time, we had all come out to the sidewalk trying to calm the man down and explain what had happened while we looked for the money. We all clarified that we were going to pay and that there was nothing to worry about even telling him we would return the pizza. Unfortunately, the police had already arrived, and with all the fuss the man had made, we didn't notice that the money had already been blown away by the wind.

The police car drove one wheel into the sidewalk and stopped. A familiar shadow opened the door and headed in our direction with a confident and resentful smile on his face. The three of us stood there, completely paralyzed, and scared down to the bone, as we recognized instantly the same horrifying glare we had encountered that Friday night when we had been witnesses of the robbery down at the jewelry shop. We knew we didn't have many options and hoped for the best. Staying as calm as we possibly could, we listened as Mr. Gordon ordered us to be quiet while the pizza deliverer told his version of the story.

"You three again, why am I not surprised," said Mr. Gordon, pinning his eyes specifically on me as he raised his thick eyebrows, trying to look over the fact that we were standing on my porch which made him look really short. Edric, Victoria and I looked at each other very alarmed but thought about how fortunate we were to have the pizza man there with us as well. It meant nothing that bad could happen. We tried to speak out calmly and explain what had really occurred after the deliverer waited for our cheap alibi. But Mr. Gordon wouldn't let us explain and needless to say, we were very unlucky, very often.

After about 15 minutes of the cold wind dancing in and out of our ears and the crazy delivery man's blabbering, Edric looked at me with those big brown eyes as if I could give him all the answers. As usual, thoughts of running away filled my mind like bees, and I couldn't feel any more frustrated and threatened by the "most respectable" figure of authority in town standing right on my doorstep.

Even with everything that was going through my head, I couldn't stop thinking about Victoria and the tremendous effort she was probably making by not having a panic attack at that very moment. I was scared too, and I was sure Edric was as well, but for Victoria, it must have been even harder to stay put. Mr. Gordon rolled his eyes and shut the pizza deliverer up with one sharp gesture and hissing sound; then he slid his evil stare back straight at us.

"Enough said! You three are going back to the station with me," he said strongly, happy to finally have a valid reason to take us with him.

Edric was standing in front of Victoria and me, he suddenly expanded his elbows to his sides in a protective manner then glued his eyes to the policeman.

Mr. Gordon took his eyes off of us for one second while he wrote in his little yellow pad about a crime we hadn't committed. Edric leaned towards my ear and whispered one word. That three letter word was our only way out: "RUN." And, that was what I did; I ran.

Victoria sped desperately behind me, and Edric followed us both, leaving the slow cop and the peculiar pizza man behind. Over sweat and anxiety, we heard the sirens coming closer and closer. We could see the police car approaching coming nearer and nearer with the pizza man in the passenger seat making our adrenaline rush even faster. That was the moment when my heart raced so fast I thought it was going to jump out into the street and run away as well, but Edric had a great idea.

"The abandoned house!" he cried. We didn't really have any time to think of another place and after all, it was our hideout. We ran as fast as our bodies would allow, and took shortcuts through areas where the police car wasn't able to fit, through little streets and alleys, over old puddles and muddy grass, leading us to the forest, which quickly lead us to the house.

We climbed the unpainted wall and then sat on the wooden porch inside, trying to calm down and recover our regular breathing and praying for the two men not to have seen us get to our hiding spot.

I looked up at the stars for a second wondering how I could be so tranquil that fast, and then at Victoria, who was looking downward and gasping for air. Finally, I glanced at Edric. His straight hair looked tangled and sweaty sticking to his face which was as red as a tomato. I dedicated a comforting smile to him and looked back up at the stars, but in a second looked right back at him coughing after a loud wheeze of frustration and astonishment, staring at what he was still holding in his hands: the stolen pizza! That was it; we were condemned. Now dreadful Mr. Gordon had evidence and a witness of our small crime. I covered my face with both hands and stared through the little holes between my fingers at Edric, trying to talk, but words wouldn't come out.

Victoria looked at me, wondering what was wrong when she finally noticed what I had a few seconds ago.

Edric looked up at both of us and then realized what he was holding in his hands, suddenly dropping it on one of the steps of the moldy porch. None of us had the words to find a solution, none of us had the answer, but we were all thinking the same thing. We were so dead! We weren't used to getting into real trouble or messing with authority, and the problem was that even if we knew we hadn't done anything, there were two much stronger adult voices against us now.

After a few endless hours, we got very hungry and decided to eat the pizza even though it was already cold. The night sky was taking over rapidly, and we were scared to come out of the house, so we decided to wait a little longer. It was a really chilly night, and we had had a terribly tiring day. I could hear toads and crickets all around us but couldn't really see any, while a cold wind fluttered through my hair and cracked my lips. After a while, we fell asleep on top of each other.

The next morning I opened my eyes and got up quickly, then wished I hadn't done it so fast since my body was all sore. I was lying against the front door alone. A bird chirped nearby, and a chill ran up my spine as a cold breeze whipped at my face.

"Victoria, Edric?" I called.

"Over here," they said.

I ran towards the voices and found them trying to get on top of the roof to see if the police car was anywhere nearby. But it was hopeless; the roof was too high, and the house had a brick wall around it so we couldn't see the panorama outside. We decided that it was time to get out. Maybe the car would have already left, or Mr. Gordon wouldn't hold that much of a grudge; maybe he wouldn't have stayed up all night just waiting for us. But I was wrong.

As we climbed the brick wall once more, I saw Victoria immediately change her smile to a terrified face. I followed her eye and looked ahead, and there it was: the police car. The officer got out of the car rapidly and grabbed my wrist really tight, probably expecting me to run away again.

"Let go of me!" I screeched, trying to set myself free. Edric's face woke up that instant, and he jumped closer to us immediately grabbing the officer's hand and letting me go from his grip. He seemed extra upset about the officer hurting me.

We were taken to the police department that same morning. The office was all dirty and smelled strangely of something like a mixture of old glazed donuts and dried up mud. There were a few other police officers walking around and chatting, holding cups of coffee with little steam clouds dancing on the surface. I was freezing cold, and seeing that hot air rise from the coffee wasn't helping. We sat down at the old, dusty couches as the secretary called each one of our parents, telling them what we had done, exaggerating the story, and, of course, explaining what our punishment would be while Mr. Gordon stood next to her desk with satisfaction written all over his face.

Well, I guess I am over-reacting a little. Doing community service is actually nice, and feeling like you help people in some way can be very refreshing. The part I did not like at all was that our parents had more faith in an old, corrupt police officer than in us; believing that we actually had the intention to steal the pizza and do all the things they said we did. At least, Mr. Gordon had had his revenge. Or, at least, that's what we thought.

2

Next week, Edric's birthday would finally arrive...17 for the win! Strangely, we were all excited except for him. I knew something was wrong.

3

Heavy raindrops fell dripping through the window and racing with each other as gravity pulled them down. The sky was gray as if it was in despair and the streets appeared empty with not one single soul wandering around. The dark clouds drifted through the wind, trying to escape the storm. I still couldn't believe that this day, Edric's birthday, could possibly have such putrid weather.

You may be wondering why we didn't do anything for his special day; I was wondering the same thing.

Suddenly, I heard something. It wasn't one of those usual noises I hear when I'm home alone, it was something completely different. My heart was pounding as if it was trying to escape my ribcage savagely. Silently I walked downstairs, trying not to move too much, holding my brother's baseball bat with both my hands, my eyes popping open as my foot reached the last step when out of nowhere, I saw him. Right in front of my eyes, it was Edric.

"How the heck did you get in here?" I asked him furiously.

He had a peculiar expression drawn on his face, one that I had never seen before; as if he had seen a ghost. Edric sat down and apologized, but didn't give me a logical explanation as to how he had managed to get inside the house at almost 12:30 pm which I thought was kind of weird, very weird actually. Judging by the look on his face, I thought it would be better to stop asking.

After a few minutes had gone by, I managed to calm him down. We sat on the floor with a couple of pillows (we rarely sit on the couch) watching one of those lame movies they put on after midnight, with a bag of salted peanuts. Edric and I ate them hungrily. After a while, we started playing with them. Edric stood up and sat down at the other end of the living room, throwing peanuts into the air to see if I was able to catch them with my mouth. His geeky laugh filled the living room as his shoulders jumped up and down. He looked upward and held his flat belly with one hand showing his almost perfect smile.

"Have you seen that new girl in school Becs?" he said in between peanut throwing.

"You mean Annie? The brunette with perfect curls?" I replied.

Edric nodded and raised his eyebrows, meaning he thought she was fairly attractive. We both laughed once more, and I playfully threw a pillow at his face.

Soon, Victoria managed to climb out of her bedroom window and join us dripping wet. I gave her a towel and my warmest nightgown. She brought some of her mother's cookies and we ate them together as I noticed Edric was coming back to his normal self. In the end, he even seemed to have forgotten whatever had happened to him a while ago, which I would probably never know.

4

It was a Friday morning. I raced to chemistry class and sat down, sweating. Mr. Sanchez had already started class, but as usual, he hadn't even noticed when I ran inside and took my seat. Erica Finch, Mr. Gordon's neighbor, had been absent again. Every morning Erica would come into class walking like a ghost and brushing her long blonde hair with her dainty, bony fingers as she sat down carrying a paper bag with blueberry muffins in it. Edric would always ask for one unsuccessfully, but he wasn't in class today either. Strange things had been happening recently, and Erica had never before been absent so many times as she had these past few weeks.

About a half hour of class had gone by and all I had written down in my notebook was a fancy title while everyone else was on their second page of formulas. I doodled on my margins and when Mr. Sanchez called on me for the third time; he popped my daydreaming bubble and threw a small piece of chalk at me, gesturing me to walk up to the board. I couldn't help but smile nervously and peak at Leonard's notebook beside me to try and figure out what was going on. Leonard and I had been friends for a while; he wasn't from around here, so his thick accent and blue eyes gave him a special characteristic. We were friends and all, but we sure liked to banter; so when he closed his notes before I could read anything else I wasn't surprised. Mr. Sanchez noticed I was a bit distracted.

"Rebecca, go get me some more chalk from room 345 please," he said, right before calling Leonard up next to finish the equation.

Mr. Sanchez gave me half a smile and let me out the door. He was my favorite teacher ever; this was just one of the many examples as to why.

After class, Victoria and I walked home as usual. "Plans for today?" she asked.

"Not for now. I think Edric wanted us to go with him somewhere," I answered.

"Where? Where is he anyway?"

I really had no clue.

Later that afternoon, we met at Joe's café. Joe's is a small, old-fashioned café sitting right next to the library. It has a way of standing out despite its simplicity. The café has a classic black and white tile floor and some beige walls clustered with sports photographs and artifacts. Of course, all the waiters wear their little sailing boat paper hats and red bandanas to keep up with the ambiance.

Stewart came close to our table wearing his shiny roller blades and his incomparable white smile.

"Same as always, Stew!" Victoria called.

"Coming right up!" he shouted back in a friendly manner as he skated away.

A couple of minutes later, two big Oreo cookie milkshakes were sitting in front of our eyes. Victoria drooled, hypnotized by the delightful masterpiece. You see, Joe's café is the best place to have a milkshake in the whole country, its proven.

All of a sudden Edric appeared leaning in a self-reliant way against our booth. He was wearing a pair of dark jeans and a smelly jeans jacket with a stained white t-shirt underneath. His hair no longer resembled a black waterfall. Instead, now it was ridgy hair with a different, darker hue which is completely difficult for me to describe. His brownish, naive eyes now looked cynical. It was quite peculiar.

"Where have you been?" Victoria asked, turning her head towards him and sculpting a frown over her heavy dark eyebrows. Edric sat next to her turbulently with his arm around her and answered in a low voice,

"Just chillin'."

He took his cap and placed it on his head facing backward in a subtle movement. Little curled up hairs sneaked from the sides; weird, but kind of attractive I guess. He looked completely different, but it went well with his facial features.

Victoria and I exchanged perplexed looks. Edric was extremely queerish lately. We had never seen him like this before. So odd, so confident, so...not himself.

After finishing our milkshakes, Edric demanded that we go with him to the store. I could tell he was afraid of something. My hands felt frozen, which always happened after being at Joe's. I rubbed them together as I heard Victoria agree to Edric's request thinking we were just going to the grocery store one block away. After practically begging us to go with him, I noticed how Edric's new-born confidence started to drain down as if suddenly he was turning back to his old self as if he was terrified of going there alone.

We walked out of Joe's with our tummies filled with ice cream when we detected that it turned out that we weren't going to the grocery store one block away; we were heading to the most dangerous suburb in our town. Edric, Victoria, and I walked down the alley rapidly, searching for the store Edric had to go to. He claimed that he had to buy some kind of curative pills for his mother. Something about him was too weird; he seemed hypnotized in a way.

Gray fumes with nasty smells sneaked out of the sewers. A gloomy atmosphere surrounded us as if someone or something didn't want us to be there. Rats ran down the streets hurriedly making squeaking noises which I hated with revulsion. Victoria grabbed my arm nervously and walked cautiously avoiding the rubble that had fallen from the decrepit brick buildings. Once more I glanced suspiciously at Edric and wondered what was really going on.

Suddenly, turning a corner of one of the streets, Edric disappeared into thin air. Victoria and I were left alone, disorientated, and mostly scared to death. Ghostlike figures appeared in the shadows formed by the nasty smog, something we didn't realize at the moment. We began to lose it as we searched desperately for a way back, or, at least, someone to talk to. We ran, afraid of everything, searching for Edric. A human-like figure appeared behind us. I knew right away it wasn't Edric; he'd be much taller. Victoria tried talking to him from a distance, forcing her eyes to try and see the face, but it was hard to see him across the mist.

The mysterious body started taking steps closer and closer, stomping a pair of very familiar black boots I knew I had seen before in a deadly quiet way. By that time, all I wanted was for that man to go away. He looked awfully suspicious; wearing a long coat and what seemed like a detective's hat. The man started sprinting out of the blue, aiming at us. Instead of trying to talk to him, we bolted away while looking back every five seconds with a small hope of a chance for him to trip or disappear. He ran faster and faster every time. Victoria and I dashed trying to escape, feeling as if our lungs were going to fall out any second. We struggled to catch our breath, trying to reach out of the fumes for clean oxygen. It was useless.

We came to a dead end, even darker than the lane in which we had been before. Panting and mostly coughing, I despairingly looked for a quick escape. That's when I eyed a rusty fire escape ladder hanging from one of the red brick buildings.

Victoria and I climbed to the top of the building as fast as we could even though I had no idea how we were going to take flight from there.

Finally reaching the roof, I pulled on Victoria, helping her up to the rooftop. I looked back down, searching for the man to try and figure out how much time we had to find a plan. The problem was that the man was no longer there. I kept looking around right beneath me and even further ahead, but could see nothing. In some way, it was kind of a relief, but it was still baffling. Where was he? We had just been a few millimeters apart. Most importantly who was he? Why was he haunting us like this? Why did he seem so, familiar? That's when I turned around to see what Victoria had been doing all this time that I had been searching for our persecutor. To my surprise, he was right there clutching her sharply in his arms with a knife slightly pushing against her white neck, wearing a pair of black woven gloves keeping me from seeing his hands.

I stood still, shocked, not knowing what to do looking at Victoria and then at that man, and back at Victoria again multiple times. I tried to find a solution in my head, but scary images of the worse that could happen flashed behind my eyes. The man handcuffed Victoria to a metal conduit and approached me very slowly with the hat shadowing his true identity. I tried to stay calm, walking backward, never unpinning my eyes from where his should be. Cornering me to the edge of the building, he got so close that I felt his body weight leaning on me. I was about to fall. He had the knife so close to my face that I could tarnish it with my breath which was coming out fiercely because of the cold and mostly because of the adrenaline running through my veins. He came one step closer, but instead of imprisoning me, or sinking the knife into my throat, he pushed me.

I fell astonishingly fast. The adrenaline ran faster; my brain kept pushing deadly images into my eyes. I could see that psychopath staring at me fall; staring to enjoy the sight of my head shattering against the concrete. I shut my eyes and swallowed my heart in one gulp.

Suddenly, I stopped falling and felt the wind gently playing around with my loose hair. Something had saved me. At that point, I was almost sure this had to be a dream. I looked up, confused, startled; it was Edric. And he was…flying? He looked back at me and forced a smile. His eyes were no longer cynical. Instead, they looked at me with guilt, but at the same time, they looked kind of, captivating. That's when it all crashed into my head like when you forget a word. You have it on the tip of your tongue, and then you finally remember it. All of these strange things that were happening. That's why Edric had been so weird since the day when he came unexpectedly to my house. Something had happened that night; that's when it had all begun.

5

We flew past the city, over the lake, and through the clouds. I looked at the stars shining above us. Edric didn't speak a word; he seemed lost in thoughts, staring straight ahead the whole time. Soon, I fell asleep in his arms.

I woke up under a moldy gray stone bridge, covered in a pile of water lilies. I saw Edric sitting on the riverbank facing the water, leaning against wooden blocks beside him. I ran towards him, discovering on the way several aching wounds and bruises I didn't have before. I called his name several times, realizing he wasn't aware of what was happening around him; as if he had been paralyzed, or hypnotized (which I thought was also a logical explanation as to why he took us to that horrible part of town in the first place). Desperately, I tried hitting him, throwing water at his face in desperation. Finally, I burst out in the tears I had been holding back. I sat down next to Edric and thought through what my possibilities were trying to get ahold of myself, trying not to feel as if I was going crazier than I already thought I was.

I examined him once again and noticed blood was still streaming down his forehead. He had been hit by something or someone. I grabbed a little pink napkin from the bakery shop that I remembered was still in the back pocket of my jeans and cleaned his wound and then sat back down.

Suddenly, I saw something weird swimming delicately beneath the surface of the water. It danced under the tiny, calm waves and around the little water lilies. My sobbing stopped for a few seconds, and my mind drifted towards figuring out what that beautiful creature was. Faded green specs of shimmering light came out of what seemed to be its scales, but I knew it wasn't a fish, it was something else.

My head couldn't stop thinking about it; hypnotized, I wanted to know what it was even though I had to figure out what to do with Edric. My hand slowly reached the water and for a second, my entire body craved the knowledge of knowing what that thing was. My fingertips were so close to touching it when a familiar hand grabbed my wrist tightly. I turned towards it alarmed, but of course, it was Edric.

I hugged Edric as hard as I could, happy to see him alive again.

"What's going on Ed? Where are we? And what happened to you?" I asked him. I continued with non-stop questions, not letting him answer any of them which was not satisfying my curiosity. He finally told me we were at a place called Lachrymose Island and that what had happened to him wasn't important. We were here because this is where Victoria was and we had to save her. He also warned me never to try and touch any living things swimming under the water but didn't explain why. He didn't say anything else, but just helped me up and walked out his sore body.

6

I was bewildered. Edric had already kind of told me what was going on, but I still didn't seem to understand anything, and he didn't seem to want me to. The only thing I could do right now was to do as he told me to, but even I knew that wasn't going to last long. He was lucky I was a little terrified or else I'd be taking the lead, as usual.

We walked along the bridge, and after that followed the river, finally drifting away from it and entering the forest.

This forest wasn't a common forest; it was like walking into a fairytale. Everything in it seemed different. Everything in it woke my curiosity, and I couldn't scratch it off. I wasn't able to focus at all.

Edric walked pretty fast, and straight forward. I couldn't stay behind, but everything in that forest seemed beautiful. I couldn't help but stop and stare. Silly monkeys played around while creatures that seemed harmless ran and jumped beside us as if we were a part of them. Giant red, smooth toads that seemed made out of porcelain hopped around the mud. What I imagined being bird noises filled the air melodically, but I wasn't quite sure they were actually birds singing. The forest was filled with life, and I loved it.

Staring at the tree tops, I tripped over a log and fell. Suddenly I noticed millions of tiny butterflies flying from inside a hole in the log. My jaw dropped open as I glared upward and admired them. They had bright, shiny white spots all around their wings, with pitch black, curled up antennas that could enchant anyone. I stayed there, just looking at those unusual butterflies.

Edric ran towards me and helped me up slowly. The butterflies surrounded us flying everywhere in an orderly manner. I had never seen anything so charming. Their light reflected every dark spot around us and even Edric's face lightened up for a change. The butterflies kept circling creating a mantle around us and pushing us closer together. We laughed and giggled, playing with the little insects and admiring their welcoming show. I never wanted it to end. One of them landed on top of Edric's nose and tickled him until he sneezed and drew the small butterfly away. But she simply joined the others as they ended their delightful performance flying upward all together to then scatter around us, raining downward in a mushroom-like pattern and then fluttering around the branches of the trees like Christmas lights.

After that fascinating moment little did I know what was going to happen next. A hard, sudden stomp hit my ears. Something wasn't right. The butterflies stopped dancing for us and flew like arrows back into the log, not giving us a chance to say goodbye.

The threatening noise kept on coming filling the air with fear and getting Edric alarmed once again. We both looked towards where the sound was coming from with eyes wide open and felt our hearts beating faster with tremor. He held my hand for a second trying to calm me down and trying to do the same for himself. He came closer and whispered once again in my ear.

"Rebecca, you have to run as fast as you can and don't look back!" I was about to ask him why not stay together when I saw the trees collapsing in the distance seeming to come closer and an animal resembling some kind of lion but with a horrid face and an abnormal amount of teeth spotting us.

We desperately ran, and ran nonstop. My feet were being pierced with tiny harmless looking rocks that had slipped into my shoes. My hair was sweaty and tangled as it hit my sides. I ran as fast as I could. It was all about surviving. My senses were all gone, and I was thinking like an animal. Thinking about getting away before the predator reached me. My legs, oh my legs! They seemed filled with adrenaline, running faster than my heart. The witty beast wildly sprung around me. Getting caught on tree branches wasn't a problem for it at all. It could get through anything, and it could destroy anything. My energy started fading away as I ran out of oxygen. I looked around for Edric. Where was he and what was I doing? Breathing was becoming a hard task for my lungs, and I didn't think I could do this for much longer.

I kept wickedly running for my life when I unexpectedly fell in a deep hole. I thought fiercely for a solution and covered my head with leaves, forgetting entirely about what could have possibly created that tunnel.

What was going on? Tears flooded my eyes once again. I was so confused and for a second I thought I was mad, imagining all these impossible things.

After a bit, I decided it was time to open my eyes again. The darkness kept me from seeing much, but I felt as if the tunnel went on forever anyway. I wondered what that tunnel really was and once again my curiosity took over. I started walking slowly inside the tunnel, guiding myself by feeling around its dirt walls when a gigantic, pink-nosed animal spotted me and chased me out. I bet he was as scared as I was. It was just a harmless mole, but a huge one. All around me was so unreal; I honestly thought I might have gone insane.

Outside once again, I feared the beast would find me, so I decided to cover myself with leaves and flowers to have a little camouflage. I walked hunched, slowly looking around to try and find Edric and also to be prepared in case I saw a slight sign of the beast reappearing, but mostly to find Edric. What could I possibly do without him? That's when the flashbacks hit me.

Edric, Victoria and I had been caught in many misunderstandings. It was as if we had a magnet for bad luck whenever we were together, but we always managed to get through it. For some reason on every occasion when I was left alone, Edric would come and find me. He had some kind of protective duty with not just me but with Victoria as well. It was pretty reassuring when I thought about it.

Looking out for Edric, the beast, holes or logs I could trip over, everything became very tiring, so I stopped. I saw an empty tree hole and sat inside it not thinking about it twice. It was better than nothing at all and it was already getting dark.

I cuddled my arms together in a secure manner under my chin and over my chest facing the outside of the tree hole. I was already falling asleep when it started raining. The rain sounded like rain, but it didn't look like ordinary everyday rain. My eyes went from being little sleepy corn seeds to open popcorn when I saw what was falling from the sky. Astonished, I held myself inside the hole with my arms wrapped around my knees but peeked out at the outside forest. I could feel a smile getting drawn across my face and my eyelashes kissing my eyebrows. The rain falling from the sky seemed to have tiny, white lights inside which faded as they got closer to the ground. It lighted up the forest, and it lighted me up as well. It was as if I'd forgotten everything that was happening for a moment. It was wonderful. After a couple of minutes, the rain looked like regular rain, but it had been something captivating to watch.

I slid back into my wooden bed and remembered a story Edric had told me once. The story about how you dream at night. I had always thought it was part of his vivid imagination; just one of his many stories, but it seemed so credible now. Edric, Victoria and I were sitting on the roof of my house one night, just looking at the cloudy, polluted sky in what could have been an uncomfortable silence for others, but not at all for us.

That night, Edric told us to look quietly through the smog and find the stars and not take our eyes away from them. He said that stars weren't what everyone said they were; that every single one of them was just a clear glass jar with a shiny dream inside, which lighted it up; and that's what we called stars. He said that every night after little kids drank their milk and went to bed, these jars would crack open and let a couple of dreams out to fill someone's head with a nice story while they slept. He said that sometimes these dreams would travel as shooting stars or would just appear on the child's head. But other times, rare times, they would travel through tiny raindrops making it rain during the night, and that was why sometimes when you'd wake up after a great dream to go out and play with your friends, you would feel wet grass under your toes.

7

I woke up with a rough hello the next morning. I scratched my eyes and stretched my feet as much as I could while still inside the little hole only to see Edric popping his head into my tree. I jumped out and hugged him feeling safe again. That's when I remembered everything that went on yesterday.

"Where did you go? We could've both gotten killed or kidnapped or eaten!" I told him, pushing his chest away. He untangled my arms gently as he usually did when I crossed them after getting mad at him and then explained how another beast had appeared, and he tried dragging them both away but only managed to distract one. He also seemed surprised about me having been able to get away from the creature that fast.

"I was worried something had happened to you," he replied. "Come on; we have to keep walking and get out of here."

I followed him feeling better now that he was with me again. We came across the biggest and oldest tree I had seen in that forest. Edric seemed extremely happy about it and told me we had to reach the top of it one way or another.

"This tree has exactly what we need," he said.

I asked him why and looked around for some way to climb it, but it was useless.

"You see Becs; this tree has some tiny bird seeds. These seeds are what help birds fly. It is what made me able to fly that day when it all started. I had been saving some in my pocket. Without these, birds would be completely disorientated and would not be able to flap their wings as they do, we could say these seeds are something like their vitamins."

I looked at him in disbelief, wrinkling the little skin between my eyebrows. But he had always been a terrible liar, so I guessed I had to believe him since he seemed credible.

"And what happens if they are far away and need more seeds?" I asked.

"These seeds are called bullets. Every bird that comes here and needs them will eat a couple and save a bunch of them in little pouches they have under their feathers. Besides, even without them, birds are able to fly, just a bit more sloppy. So we have to get some for ourselves. We are the only living thing on this island, apart from birds that are capable of reaching them."

We tried everything: Climbing, jumping, getting on each other's shoulders; but nothing worked. It seemed impossible. We sat down in the dirt and thought of things we could do. Little pink crickets hopped around Edric's right foot,

"Ugh I hate crickets," he said as he shook his leg.

"I know you do," I told him.

That's when I remembered summer two years ago. Edric had gone to a wilderness survival and fun camp. The day he came back Victoria and I took him to Dibblers'. I remembered him complaining about how much he hated crickets and how they would sometimes get in his bed at night. I also remembered how he told us they had learned how to make fish nets with pure forest materials, learning how to fish salmon from the creek and cooking it for dinner every night.

"That's it!" I told him.

"Ed, we have to build a fish net and catch the next bird that flies off of the tree."

Edric looked at me a little confused.

"We can build a fish net; you know how to do that, then just maybe make it a little longer and catch one of the birds to get some of the seeds it keeps in its feathers. We won't do anything to it; I mean, it can always fly back up and get more."

Edric was skeptical about it but agreed to follow my idea since he couldn't think of anything better.

"There are some things you should know before we start the plan," he said.

"Every afternoon when the sun starts going down, flocks of birds fly over and get their provisions for the week. It can get a little dangerous, but it can also be our only chance of getting this right. There are so many things that could and probably will go wrong, but okay Becs, let's do this." he said.

"This is what we will need."

After a few hours, we finished building what was now a bird catcher. Edric took it and climbed another tree that was pretty tall too right next to the bullet tree. Not knowing what else to do I climbed it behind him trying to catch up but falling back down. I had forgotten how athletic and different Edric had become after his birthday some days ago. As much as I tried and wanted to, climbing trees wasn't really my thing.

Waiting was boring. I hadn't been bored at all since we got here and it was a little frustrating. What if this plan didn't even work? I sat In the dirt once again playing around with tiny flowers and pebbles.

We heard thunder in the distance. I shrieked and looked up at Edric. He looked back down at me and told me not to worry giving me that calming look he gives me. Creepy, gray clouds made their way into the forest, making it seem even darker than it already was. I started feeling raindrops on my face but didn't stop looking at Edric. I was kind of waiting for him to tell me what we would do next. Edric shouted loudly explaining how when there was a thunderstorm, not every bird came to get bullets so we would have to deal with whatever did come.

These raindrops weren't like the one's I had seen the night before. These seemed gloomy and dark, scary as well. It almost seemed as if the raindrops had feelings. Suddenly, I heard something else over the sound of the rain. I looked around and saw an army of black birds coming towards the tree.

"Edric they are coming!" I screamed, jumping back on my feet.

"Are you ready?" hollered Edric back at me. I nodded and faced towards the birds ready for anything. These creatures looked more like bats with fangs and bloodcurdling faces.

The bats surrounded the tree creating a black drape. Edric's hair flew everywhere, and I could barely see him, and I knew he could barely see me. The animals flew in and out, around, and on top of us. It was as if they were desperate for these seeds. As if these seeds were a drug to them; as if the seeds would run out. It was hard to stay calm as the heavy gusts of wind and flapping wings disoriented my balance.

Edric raised the bird catcher with one arm holding himself with the other and swung it all around trying to catch a bat while keeping more from getting in as well as keeping the one he caught from flying out. But it was useless. Standing up had already been hard enough for me with all the ataxia and confusion these birds were causing. So the fact that I was knocked out by Edric falling on top of me wasn't amusing. It all happened so fast I barely even noticed. Maybe he was stronger, more agile and different, but somewhere inside his flesh he was still that clumsy little boy.

8

My head felt heavy and fat as if it was about to fall off. Getting the hair off of my face and dirt off of my hands, I remembered what had happened the night before. I stood up quickly; then I wished I had done so gently because of all the scratches from the wings of the bats and how much they ached. Edric was nowhere in sight. The tree was still there, but the clouds were gone as well as the bats who had left behind a trail of black feathers and a couple of corpses too. I screamed Edric's name and walked around a little, discovering new scratches and cuts all over my skin with each step.

I saw Edric unconscious, lying on the other side of the tree. I sat next to him and smoothened his hair a little, playing with it a bit too. I then began to wipe the blood off his face with a scrap of cloth I had ripped from my sleeve, hoping he wouldn't wake up too pissed. I knew how upset he'd be that our plan didn't work, just as much as I was. He opened his eyes slowly brushing my hand off of his face as he sat up next to me. I could see the discouragement in his face; he clearly really wanted those seeds, and I knew how much we needed them.

I looked right at him and told him we would find a way to cross the island without using these seeds. I explained that he had my full support and I would do anything he told me to do and follow his instructions as best as I could.

Edric half smiled at me and picked a lilac flower from a tiny bush growing around the roots of the tree. He placed it behind my ear as he said, "Those who really want to help for good will be helped for good as well."

He got up with the confidence I'd given him and reached down to help me up too. I looked once again at the flowers under the tree just to admire them one last time. But suddenly I noticed something I hadn't before. I kneeled down, moving some dirt and leaves and saw four little seeds sitting there beneath the flowers.

I grabbed them rapidly and jumped right up again showing them to Edric, who was right behind me trying to peek and see why I had kneeled down in the first place. His half smiled brightened into a full one. He grabbed the seeds laughing right before hugging me and lifting me in the air.

"This might feel a bit weird," he warned me. "The first time I tried it I didn't know what to do or how to move. You gotta have lots of patience and coordination as well."

Edric gave me two of the seeds keeping the other two for himself and told me to chew and then swallow. I examined them, still unconvinced about everything, but then just put them in my mouth hurriedly and did as Edric told me without hesitating any longer.

I felt a very peculiar taste in my mouth. It was hard to chew at first, but then it just took on a caramel type texture that would get stuck everywhere around your mouth; except it didn't taste like caramel at all. Yet, who wouldn't want to chew magical seeds that made you fly? But honestly, they couldn't have tasted any worse. I looked at Edric in disgust immediately as if looking for an explanation of why he hadn't told me before that these things tasted this bad as I tried to finish chewing. I felt my nose wrinkling and the corners of my lips going downward as I shut my eyes hard and squished Edric's wrist. Even he, who had had those terrible seeds before couldn't help but make faces in front of me while trying to hide the bitterness of the situation which wasn't something he was especially good at.

I finished swallowing and gave him a little whack, still feeling the bitter after-taste all around my taste buds.

"You'll get used to it," he said, as he exhaled and snickered softly. I could see the excitement in his eyes.

What happened next was a bit scary. All of a sudden I started floating away from the floor. I looked down at the pebbles beneath me with eyes wide open and thought I might just be dreaming. But Edric took my hand, floating a bit higher than me and gave me assurance without saying anything. He signaled me easily how all this worked and how to drift from side to side, upward or downward. It wasn't hard at all to get the hang of it.

How flying felt is impossible to describe. I couldn't believe what was going on at that moment. It was, of course, something you only dream of doing, and right now I was living it. I bet my smile had never been bigger. Edric looked at me and smiled back with joyous eyes. His short hair barely moved in the wind while mine went everywhere without bothering me at all. We went higher and higher, moving fast above the trees.

We reached the clouds and twirled around them, losing sight of each other for small instants but reappearing through the fluff once again. We then raced down towards the Lachrymose Lake, and I slid my fingers over the water creating funny patterns and filling my lungs with fresh air. I could feel my laughter roaring louder than I could actually hear it or Edric's. All the excitement I was feeling was uncontrollable. Even if we had to get to our destination faster and had no time for games, I'm sure it was the most fun I had ever had.

I could feel the strong wind all over my body but also the warmth of the sun rays on my skin.

All of a sudden, I saw Edric disappear under some treetops. "Follow me; I have to show you something!"

I followed his voice and drifted towards where I'd heard it disappearing under the branches. I spotted him right away and flew faster, reaching his right foot and pulling it backward playfully as I got ahead of him.

"Keep going forward!" he screamed.

I did as he told me and kept going just to find the most beautiful thing I had ever seen. As the light started getting brighter and the forest came to an end, I stopped flying instantly looking at what was the most jaw-dropping scene I could have imagined. Edric knew how much I loved sunflowers and tulips; well anyone who has ever seen my doodles on any of my notebooks would know that. The endless flower field went up the mountain side and reached everything I could see from that spot. There wasn't one thing that wasn't covered in flowers. The field was so carefully divided, some spots flourishing with colorful tulips, other spots bursting with the yellow petals of sunflowers. It looked like someone had just dropped different colors of paint everywhere. I chuckled and covered my mouth just to see Edric fly into the scene with a huge smile on his face. I followed him once again and noticed little butterflies and bees flying around making patterns in the wind as if they were happy as well; as if they were happy to see us.

I never wanted this to end, but I knew it had to. Eventually, the effect had worn off, and we had run out of seeds. Edric and I had to walk once again; but it wasn't as bad, we had cut a very long way in just a few minutes. Of course, what we had just lived was something I could never ever forget.

Never had I experienced my body getting so flooded with all that adrenaline. I turned a red tulip around my fingers as we continued our way, talking nonstop about the past few hours and how everything had felt; still very excited. Edric, on the other hand, began feeling very bitter and started getting in a gloomy mood again. His mood had changed a lot since the incident around his birthday weekend, and I knew that he tried to stay calm anyway, but it wasn't the same. He asked me to shut up about it and concentrate on what we had to do; so I did.

9

After walking for what seemed hours, we got to a beach that seemed very familiar. It was wide with white sand and turquoise water that seemed to attract you instantly. I noticed how an arrangement of green bushes, trees and leaves trimmed the side of the beach which made it even more familiar. A refreshing wind blew on my face with a salty smell that stayed trapped around my hair. I grabbed my shoes; my feet felt relieved after pressing against the cold sand. Edric, on the other hand, didn't seem impressed at all, he just kept walking ahead.

"Edric," I said. "Why don't we rest here for a bit? We could stay here for a while and maybe swim a little and get all this dirt off of us."

Edric glanced at me, gestured a hard no and kept walking straight. He had changed so much with such short notice; he wasn't that awkward little boy anymore. I followed him, not saying another word. I figured if he said no then there might have been a good reason to listen to him.

After a while, I decided I was going to stay for a little bit. I deserved a break from all of this for at least a few seconds. I quickly placed my shoes on the sand, and jumped into the water, not bothering to tell Edric anything; I didn't think, I didn't care, I just wanted some time to clear my head and forget about all this; just a few minutes, that was all I asked for. He wouldn't even notice my absence anyway. Plus I could just get in, clean up a bit and get back out, no big deal.

I saw Edric for an instant after I was floating above the clear water, not a single wave bothered me. I then saw how he noticed I wasn't behind him anymore. He seemed to be running towards the water trying to tell me something, but I couldn't hear what it was, and I honestly and stupidly didn't think it was something urgent. It could certainly wait; so I breathed in a big gulp of air and swam back in.

The water felt cold at first, but then it just felt like it was part of me. Have you ever seen those chocolate commercials where melted chocolate just slides delicately over a cookie? Well, that's how it felt. I wanted to stay there forever and didn't even feel the need to go up for air anymore.

I swam deep. Maybe there were wicked mermaids or peculiar animals around me, but the feel of the water made me forget.

I felt almost asleep; so relaxed and as nonchalant as one could ever be. Every muscle, every cell in me was turned off. The water made me feel safe; so when a thick, unpredictable rope tightened harshly around my stomach and pulled me roughly out of the water, I couldn't have been more alarmed and scared.

10

We were walking to the Vile Fair rapidly. I know it was probably dangerous for Rebecca, but we had to get there. After everything that had been happening, she seemed clueless, and I really didn't have time to explain anything yet. But we really had to get there before sundown. Crossing the beach to get there seemed like a good idea. Rebecca was suddenly calmed down with the sound of the small waves crashing on the shore and the sand in her toes which was good. Even if I knew those waters were very dangerous indeed, I thought I could keep her out of them and cross the beach quickly.

Of course, I couldn't keep her from being her curious self for long. I was leading the way, as usual, encouraging her to walk faster when she decided to stop.

"Edric," she told me. "Why don't we rest for a while? We could stay here for a bit and maybe swim a little."

I looked at her for a quick second; not wanting to be mean I gave her a short glance and kept walking, gesturing her to follow me as we had been doing before. She might have been tired and everything, but we really had to hurry; this part of the island is filled with mysteries.

Rebecca was honestly getting on my nerves already. I had been noticing how lately it was hard for me not to get mad at her; how every little thing she did bothered me even if it was something good. And it wasn't just her, everything around me bothered me too much, and I didn't know why.

After a few minutes, I noticed I couldn't hear her shoes squeaking against each other like they had been doing when she walked as she held them in her left hand. I looked behind me, and she wasn't there anymore. I rolled my eyes and asked myself how this hadn't crossed my mind before; I mean, it's Rebecca we are talking about after all.

I took a quick look around and then noticed her shoes there lying on the sand, I looked around a little more and saw she had gotten into the water; after everything that had happened, she would finally see me panic. These waters were the most unknown waters on the island; there could be anything in there, and she didn't know that. I tried calling her name, screaming; waving my arms into the air, but nothing seemed to get her attention. I would have to get in too, and get her out of the trance she appeared to be stuck in.

I ran towards the water as I took my shirt and shoes off at the same time when I noticed a pirate ship. These island pirates weren't like the ones you would think; these are completely psychotic, and of course much more dangerous indeed. I was sure the pirates would get her and of course, I would have to save her.

Shocked at the sight of this, I had to do something. I couldn't fly right now and swimming towards her would just get them another easy prey, but I had to do something! I couldn't just let her get caught like that, so I decided I would get in.

As I started swimming deeper and deeper as fast as I could, I saw them rope catching her. It was too late now. I would have to find another way to get her. How could I have been so stupid? How could

I have not warned her? I had been so focused on getting us out of that island and finding Victoria that I didn't think of how she felt or what things she might do. I knew her better than that.

My feet were cold, and my mouth was dry. I felt so worried about her; first Victoria, and now her. What was I going to do know? I couldn't bear the thought of losing them both. And Rebecca; she had been through so much confusion since we got here which surely didn't compare to Victoria being kidnapped which was also terrifying.

Not knowing what to do and trying not to alarm myself, even more, I started thinking about what my options were as the pirate ship made its way into deeper and deeper currents.

I sat down on the sand, pushing my head against my hands and shutting my eyes as hard as I could hoping to think of something quick. All the time we were here, I tried my best to make Rebecca believe that I knew this island like the palm of my hand so that she would feel safer, but the truth is that I barely know the basics; that was scary.

The original plan to find Victoria was to go and look for her at the Vile Merchants Fair, which was where all the pirates and shopkeepers would go and exchange goods. Maybe her kidnapper would be there. That was exactly where I'd go to find them both.

It had all gotten so complicated. Everything had changed so fast, and I couldn't even think of what the girls would say and how I could start explaining everything.

The beach seemed endless. I kept running forward, hoping to get to the fair fast but it was harder than I thought. The sun rays were getting stronger than usual, and my feet felt heavier with every step I took. To top it off, my stomach was about to devour itself from how hungry I was feeling. I sat down on the sand for just a minute or two trying not to panic, thinking about a plan. The sun was hot indeed, but the sand felt cool. I stuck my fingers in it and found cold on the bottom; it felt pretty refreshing. Sweat ran downward tickling my spine, all around my neck and over my forehead not letting me breathe in deep. But as I laid my raw back against the sand, I felt a little bit more relaxed. The anger inside me was cooling off a little bit which was good. I knew it would overflow any minute if I didn't do anything about it. I closed my eyes and felt the cool breeze and the sun rays cooking my chest and arms when I decided it was best to go look for something to eat now.

Finding food was not hard at all. I walked away from the shore towards the forest and found a banana tree surprisingly fast right in front of me. A couple of monkeys swung around the trees beside me, but they didn't seem to be bothered by my presence, and I wasn't bothered by theirs. For some reason, having monkeys like these around me wasn't amusing at all. I didn't really care about these things; although I knew Rebecca would've gone crazy with them, just how she felt when we were flying. I had fun, yes, but it wasn't something that chatterbox had to talk so much about. The problem was, this indifference that I was developing hadn't always been there, and since my birthday a couple of days ago it had only grown stronger.

11

Stepping one foot into the Vile Fair was already too eerie, especially when you got there at sundown. The air felt thick and cold even if the place was filled with people and things. Smoke from cigars and pipes would sneak into my lungs and cause them to afflict a little. Everything was just too bothersome in a scary way.

There was a big arch at the entrance of the fair which was standing at the far end of the pier. The wooden arch seemed as if it would plummet any second; its aged light bulbs buzzed and screeched as their tired lights faded at times which was the last thing you'd notice because of how many rats and spider webs decorated the venue. Everything was dark; everything was gloomy; I had to gulp twice before I finally stepped inside.

Ironically, this fair wasn't meant for children or any person who wasn't looking for trouble. I was worried about Rebecca, but I was also thankful that she wouldn't have to witness this nerve wrecking sight.

I strutted, trying not to stand out as much. Mischievous chuckles, drunken confabulations, fists clenching before hitting someone in the face all filled my eardrums queerly. Even if everyone here was minding their own business, I could feel bitter frowns following me and painful stares sticking to the back of my neck.

I walked into what looked like an old canteen and tried to act as slick as possible as I approached the bartender. He didn't seem as mean; maybe he knew something. The place was too dirty, and it felt unclean to even breathe the air around me. Maybe the fact that it was filled with drunken customers made it even worse. I walked slowly, very carefully, watching my every move as the wooden floors screeched with every step I took lifting a small amount of dust within them. The good thing was that between the small talk, the bar fights and the alcohol, it was easy to blend in without anyone really spotting me there. I noticed how there was one lady sitting at the bar, the only one in sight. I smiled at her and stared for a while. She had thick golden locks and skin whiter than the marshmallows we usually bought for movie nights. Her scarlet outfit, big hat covering her eyes, and matching dress made her so picturesque she seemed like she had been taken out of some kind of superhero comic strip: "The Damsel in Distress" perhaps. It was rare to see such a fine lady sitting in a place like this. But when I was about to talk to her, I hadn't yet said a word when I noticed the fangs peering out under her lips as she chuckled at a slightly funny joke one of the guys around her had performed.

My eyes popped out when I saw such a thing. This was something I had only seen inside a horror movie screen; something I always thought was unrealistic. My hands felt cold and sweaty as I sat a couple of seats away from her.

The bartender, probably the only one who wasn't drunk, saw my anguish instantly and was the first one to tell I wasn't from around here. He raised one eyebrow and got closer to me placing his left arm on the counter and squishing a cockroach that ran down his beard with his right hand. I tried not to feel sick about this and managed to stay calm. The bartender got so close to my face that I could tell what he had had for lunch. His yellow teeth showed as he smiled maliciously at me.

"Fresh prey," he murmured, scrunching his yellow teeth against each other.

I squinted my eyes and tried to ignore his threatening voice as I thought of something to say. I swallowed my fear in one notorious gulp and pulled myself together again.

"So uh, tuna salad huh?" I whispered a bit too loud, trying to sound funny and figured no one would hear me anyway.

As usual, I was wrong. As soon as those words slipped out of my mouth, even the three-armed piano man stopped playing his background music and pulled his hat up to see me. I felt so intimidated; frozen. I desperately looked around for an escape. I guess foreigners aren't welcome here.

I stood up slowly trying not to stumble upon those piercing eyes and made my way to the door walking backward, afraid of disconnecting my eyes from all those people who I could tell didn't like me one bit. Finally reaching my escape, I smiled faintly before I dashed out the door. I kept walking deeper inside the fair and noticed how everyone just stared at me as if I was some kind of circus freak, but it didn't really matter because I also noticed that as long as I didn't make eye contact with anyone, then I wouldn't get into any trouble.

Standing in a corner alone, there was an old man with a white stained paper hat on his head behind what seemed to be a cotton candy stand. He didn't look as mean. In fact, I decided to ask him some questions since he seemed to know at least a little more than I did. I was already slowing down my pace under the white street light that illuminated his tin cart; when one of the witches cut me off in the line. She didn't look like much of a witch at first. You see, witches are not as you picture them in fairy tales with green faces and black hats. Sometimes they might just look like hideous women in ordinary gowns. She giggled uncontrollably for a few seconds and then in a quick instant turned her face into one big beautiful smile and changed her tone of voice completely. She now looked like a younger version of herself, young and fairly attractive.

"One cotton candy with fly sprinkles please," she announced in an innocent but annoying manner.

She twinkled her eyelashes and played with her hair in an act of trying to hide her ugly face and, even more, morbid intentions. The almost nice salesman gave her the cotton candy, faking a half smile. And as she walked away confidently, she bumped harshly into my shoulder. The salesman called her back asking her to pay, frowning and gesturing a "come back ma'am" with his right hand. I could see the witch rolling her eyes and turning around harshly. Without saying a word, she looked at him straight in the eye, and after he had finished guessing what his awful future would be, she turned him into a spider with a simple flick of her finger and threw him on top of her cotton candy. She smiled and winked at me as she said that a little extra sprinkles on her treat were always well received. I quickly backed out of her way and saw her maniacally laughing and walking back to get her broom at the closet of quick transportation. Who knows if it even was her broom? And why was I even talking about brooms? All of this had been so shocking I wasn't sure if maybe I was having some kind of hallucination or if I had just been having night terrors.

I couldn't believe what I had just seen. You might think I know a lot about this world because maybe sometimes that's what it seems like; but not at all. Every hour and each minute you spend here you get to see or find out something entirely new. This is sometimes something amazing and helpful, but sometimes you wish you didn't know anything at all.

The crowd around me seemed taken out of a nightmare or horror story; witches, pirates, freaks, vampires, werewolves, loons and maniacs wandered around. Without announcement, a white skeleton-like hand clenched my wrist and pulled me over downward to meet his stare. The short man had a curled black mustache, all ruffled and dirty. He had a striped piece of cloth tied around his head, and stains of something I couldn't figure out all over his white tank top.

I looked at him in disgust and releasing my hand from his, I asked what he wanted and checked my pockets hastily to see if anything was misplaced. He spoke in an uncanny tone, and while playing with a slimy toad around his fingers, he told me he could help me find what I was looking for.

I looked straight at him; he paused and looked back at me turning his mischievous smile into half a frown, shoving the toad back into one of the filthy jars sitting on what I figured was his merchandise table.

"Go on," I said.

The skeletal man indicated me to follow him into his little hut. I was desperate and had to do anything to find Victoria and now Rebecca too, so I did.

12

The moldy door was very small, and I had to stoop to get in. I walked inside very cautiously looking all around trying not to stare too much at all the eerie things sitting around me. Judging by how small the place looked like at first, I was surprised as to how big it seemed once you were inside. I walked behind the man making sure he didn't pull any tricks on me and got caught in a couple of spider webs. I looked up following the webs and spotted vast amounts of arachnids on the ceiling. I tried not to think about it and kept moving forward.

We got to the far end of the shed where there was a wooden table with some blocks of wood around it and a fireplace in the corner giving us a glow of light. Not quite sure of what to do, I pulled out one of the chunks of wood and took a seat placing my hands on the table waiting to see what would happen next. The man reached out for a rusty metal box sitting on the far top of a shelf and sat across the table facing me blowing away the dust decorating the box. He placed the box in front of me and told me he knew what I was looking for; I looked at him in disbelief.

"What do you mean?" I asked him.

It was very hard to believe what he was saying. After all, people around here do anything and say anything to trick you all the time.

"First of all," he said just giving me a quick glance. "My name is Paul, so call me that from now on. Now, I know yours is Edric, am I right?"

His sneaky smile slithered down his face once more as he noticed how perplexed I felt that he actually knew what my name was.

"Yes," I replied hastily trying to sound confident after I realized he knew more about me than I thought. Then again, he knew I needed help from the beginning.

It was hard not to stare at him; his spine curled in as he sat in a hunchbacked manner. I could see his vertebrae jumping upwards. It was eerie, yet fascinating. I had never seen someone like this before.

Paul finally opened the box, but I couldn't see inside it since he purposely covered its insides from me with his elbow and using the box's lid as well. I was surprised when a sudden gust of wind came out of the little box and hit his face. He grunted and kept doing what he was doing when the wind stopped. Paul put both his hands inside the box, and I noticed he started looking for something specific. That metal box was so little, yet he could put his entire head inside it along with his arms. I heard clinging and things falling as he searched for what he wanted to find. I could swear I even saw a rat running out of the box too. It was like a big closet submerged in a tiny container. Funny how everything around here is so full of magic and still has believability as well once you get to see it.

After a few minutes, Paul pulled out what seemed like an antique bottle. It was really oxidized and blackened with time, but it reminded me of my grandmother's perfume collection.

His eyes lit up, enchanted by the peculiar object. Not wanting to interrupt his thoughts, I waited patiently for him to say something before I did. Then, he drew his stare over to me, scanning me in silence. What's supposed to happen now? I thought to myself.

"Do you have anything that belongs to them?" he asked.

"What do you mean?" I replied.

Paul rolled his eyes and stood up in his seat bouncing a little.

"Do you have anything that belongs to your missing friends?" he said loudly and irritated.

His little fangs and missing teeth caught my eye for a second.

"Uh, yes yes I do," I told him as I handed him Rebecca's shoes I had been carrying around all this time. I knew these were her favorites, and I didn't want to leave them on the beach.

"What about the other girl?"

I once again wondered how he knew so much about this as I checked my pockets for something that belonged to Victoria, but it was useless.

"It's okay," he said. "They are probably being held captive together, so we will be able to see both of them."

Paul grabbed one shoe and held it close to his face. He then opened his mouth wide and hastily chewed the end of one of the shoelaces, ripping it apart and tossing the shoe back on the table. Then, he shook the aglet, cleaning it a little bit from his thick saliva and carefully slid it inside the glass container.

We waited one, maybe two seconds. I was amazed as I watched how the little object started lighting up all by itself. It was pure magic. Paul's face grew in amazement too even though I was sure he had used this unusual gadget before. But it was truly something to watch.

The light seemed to compact slowly all together inside the bottle forming tiny bubbles, and little by little it started floating towards its opening. After that, the light came out gently in what seemed like one soap bubble. It was so bright it lit up our faces and seemed so rich in light that it could have been a little crumble from the sun. I was so amused by what I was seeing, my eyes were not able to blink, and my mouth dropped open ready for bugs to fly in. Even if that did happen, I'm sure I wouldn't even have noticed it.

When the bubble got to our eye level, the light inside it started shifting letting us see little by little a blurry image that would get clearer and clearer. I burst in a mixture of excitement and fear when I saw both my friends tied up, back to back, crying their eyes out on a wooden floor. My heart sunk when I saw them. I couldn't see them like this. I was filled with despair and not able to do anything about it. My eyes filled with anger and guilt for bringing them into this. I felt so powerless and tied up myself. I had to do something right away; I had to find them.

I got up and took handfuls of my short hair attempting to pull it out to the sides and glancing upwards trying to hold my desperation.

"Where are they?" I asked.

Paul looked at me and silently gestured me to keep watching.

"Juliet," he whispered without unlocking his eyes from the scene.

I slid my knee on my stool again but stayed up; I wasn't able to stay still for one more second.

"Juliet? What is that? What are you talking about?" I said loudly, looking for answers quick.

"That's the name of the ship kid, and it's not good news."

I knew something was wrong; even Paul did. But, at least, the compassion in his eyes told me he would be willing to help with whatever he could.

13

Victoria was screaming for her life. She pushed and kicked anyone who got near her. She moved rapidly and stubbornly, but it was useless. Suddenly, we got tied up together and were thrown down the stairs. As I got the hair out of my eyes, I heard the small door being shut and locked above us.

Victoria and I were glad to be together at last, but agony won us over as we looked upon our situation. She started weeping and lamenting herself in a loud manner. I could feel her slouching over and bending trying to guide her hands to wipe her sorrowful eyes. I tried to talk to her and tell her everything was going to be fine even though I did not believe one bit of what I was saying myself. She stopped crying for a second and realized that even if she had been there alone all this time, at least now she had me with her. Then, she would realize I was indeed with her again and cried even more because I was stuck in there with her as well. About half an hour went by and Victoria was still mournfully sobbing. I seriously do not know how her eyes didn't dry out after all this. A loud bang was heard on the door, and an old petulant voice demanded Victoria to shut her mouth or, "she would have to walk the plank and jump as a snack to the sea creatures." Of course, this only caused Victoria to feel even more desperate and caused her to cry even louder.

Everything around us was very basic and made out of wood. Hot like an oven, I could feel the sweat running down my cheeks and around the gaps of my blouse finally reaching the back of my jeans. The sticky ambiance was definitely not helpful.

After a few hours, I managed to calm Victoria down. Her tired eyes had won her over making her fall asleep leaning against my clavicle. A few tears were still rushing quietly along my cheeks, but I could hide them well, and Victoria had not noticed before since her loud sobbing covered my quiet cries. It was easy to calm her down and make her believe it wasn't as bad as it seemed. Misery was taking over my thoughts as I was just sitting there, waiting for someone to come save me; waiting for something to happen. But these monsters that had caught us could never be called humans. They were nasty but stupid. That's when I thought I had to save myself and my best friend.

Desperately, I looked around for solutions to get out. After all, I was Rebecca; I was indeed the valiant hero I had dreamed of in my sleep. I could be that person. I was able to control myself and figure something out. The room was dark, but the good news was that even though the door above us was locked, there was no one else inside with us.

I scanned the room and spotted some kerosene lamps lining the wall. If I could somehow get a hold of one of them, I could smash it against the man's head. I looked at the trap door above me and pictured someone opening it, picturing how and where and how hard I should aim to throw it.

That night it was impossible to sleep thinking of ways to escape and about what could happen and why we were being held captive made it a nightmare. Victoria woke up nervous and quickly asked me how long she had been asleep. I told her approximately a couple of hours. My wristwatch had died as soon as we got to the island and keeping track of time was very hard in our situation.

The waves made us rock from one side to the other, and I was feeling very seasick as was Victoria. I told her about my escape plans and she agreed, but first, we had to try and untie ourselves.

The rocking of the boat we were trapped in started getting heavier and heavier, flipping our empty stomachs. I could tell it was past midnight already. The moonlight pierced in through the cracks of the wooden floors on top of us and there seemed to be no movement or cursing from the pirates at all which felt pretty calming. I had also managed to loosen the grip of the rope a little so Victoria and I could, at least, look at each other now. As she sat up straight and pulled her head up, she looked me in the eyes and hugged me as best as she could, placing her head on my shoulder, releasing a couple of extra tears.

Suddenly, we heard the trap door open. We looked at the stairs alarmed, ready for anything when we noticed it wasn't a threat at all. A handsome young boy around our age seemed to be sneaking in with us holding a paper bag wrapped under his arms. He looked around quickly making sure no one had seen him and closed the little trap door behind him as he walked down the stairs. He was tall with delightful blue eyes and short white blonde hair covered partly with a black bandana. He was wearing black pirate boots and cinnamon pants with a baggy white shirt halfway opened that fell gently over his upper body, covered in all kinds of stains. But that didn't stop him from being the most charming figure we had seen in a while.

"Don't scream, please," he said as he came closer little by little.

He seemed to be as scared of us as we were of him or anyone in that boat really. I sat up straight and pulled myself up in front of Victoria trying to look as strong and big as I could.

"Who are you, and what do you want with us?" I said, straightforward scanning him for any kind of weapon.

"Listen," he said as he left the bag on the floor and raised his arms upward for us to see he wouldn't harm us.

"I'm here to help; please listen to me. My name is Jimmy. I've been in this boat for quite a while. In fact, I was born here right before my mother passed away and I have always wanted to leave this place. I know there's something out there I gotta find, but it's hard. These blokes are all over me all the time, so I can't really just walk away. But I'm going to tell you somethin'; I do not think like em'. This is not right, and I won't let em' do anything to either of youse. Bloody oath!"

"Alright Jimmy, let us out then!" said Victoria, with a gulp of confidence I had rarely seen in her.

"Holy Dooley! If I could, I would have let yer pretty faces out already, but it's not as easy as it appears. If I can't escape myself, it's even harder to let you out too. If I do, we will all get killed at once. But for now, I'll be sure to bring a tucker-bag for both of you every night after the captain is

off his face. Even some lollies once in a while too!" he replied, showing his white, perfect smile, glancing at both of us before locking his eyes to Victoria's.

She smiled back at him and at me too. I guess we could somewhat trust him.

"Jimmy, where are you from? Why do you talk like that?" I asked him.

"I could barely understand what you just said."

He chuckled and looked up at us as he took his bandana off and ran his fingers through his hair.

"I meant to say that as soon as the captain gets drunk and passes out every night, I'll make sure to bring down a bag of food for you, and if I manage to get em,' some caramels too. And as I said before, I was born here on this bloody boat but the bastard who raised me as an ankle biter was Australian. He claimed to be my father and took care of me until he passed away a short while ago. That old bloke taught me all I know. He defended me and taught me that there's a life away from all this. Because of that, I've grown speakin' with a mixture of accents and words from him and the other men around here. But I'll make an effort to speak more like you from now on."

Victoria and I glanced at each other thankful to know we had a guardian angel on this dreadful boat. But at the same time, I wasn't sure we could fully trust him. Why couldn't he just leave? Let us out and take us away? Maybe he was right, and we could all die if we tried, but we couldn't afford to stay here forever either. As if having read my thoughts, Victoria spoke up again.

"It's awfully nice of you to want to help us, Jimmy," she said. "But I can't fully understand why we can't just leave. Are we staying here forever?"

Jimmy looked at her with compassion as he noticed her voice starting to crack.

"Look, just like you, I'm trapped on this same boat. These hoons expect me to be part of them or die. I can't just leave and take all the ship's secrets with me; they wouldn't let me do that, I know too much. Even if I disagree with everything my mates do and the orders they follow, if I leave I'm dead, and I won't let that happen to you either. We can't leave, at least not till we figure somethin' out." he explained as he opened the bag he had brought with him.

Orders they follow, I thought to myself. What orders? From who? I wanted to ask Jimmy but preferred to stay quiet and keep it to myself. I'd find out eventually. Besides, there was no need to put more information out there before we managed to handle all we had on our plate for now. Jimmy seemed nice, and he wouldn't let us starve

71

to death. We would probably be able to figure out a plan eventually when our friendship grew stronger.

Jimmy untied us right after telling us not to blast away with the intention of escaping because then the three of us would be caught up in even bigger problems. I figured he was right, especially because if we were lucky enough not to get caught again, we would have to jump into the water with who knows what creatures eyeing us from beneath the waves. He carefully placed the rope next to him setting us free but told us he would have to tie us again before leaving in case anyone else came down to check on us. I massaged my swollen wrists noticing all the rope bruises like bracelets that had been tattooed from all the tugging. Victoria did the same looking anxiously at me. I hugged her again and then looked back at Jimmy.

"Why are we here?" I asked.

"I'm not quite sure, Sheila. Someone must've given the captain orders to get both of you for a fair amount of moolah. As I said before, the sailors in this mob usually follow orders," he replied.

"Ok, first of all, my name is Rebecca, not Sheila. And what even is moolah?"

I was getting irritated by all this nonsense and raised my voice loud enough to then realize it had been a mistake; someone could have heard us.

"Becs I think moolah means money," whispered Victoria into my ear loud enough for Jimmy to hear.

He smiled and confirmed she was right also explaining that by Sheila he meant to get my attention. He said Sheila meant girl. We all laughed for the first time in a long time as we chatted and compared each other's vocabulary. I figured Jimmy hadn't had that much of a good time in a while either. He pulled out three smelly squid sandwiches from the bag and some apples too. Victoria smelled hers in a queerish way and took a small bite a little unsure despite how much her stomach had been roaring earlier. Jimmy took big savage bites and cleared the crumbles around his mouth with his white sleeve carelessly before taking the next bite, not showing any manners or compassion towards the poor little sandwich. Victoria and I stared at him and then we looked at each other and smiled, as we told ourselves we weren't home anymore deciding to enjoy our peculiar dinner too. We ate the sandwiches and nibbled on the apples as Victoria and I shared all that had happened and how our lives were back home and about Edric too.

Time flew by. We spent all night chatting and forgot about everything that was going on, and, before we knew it, the sunlight drilled its way through the cracks in the wood as the starry sky faded into a pinkish- yellowish palette like the ones I used back home to paint. Jimmy panicked as he took all the evidence of the food and placed the rope around us hurriedly. He told us to make sure no one noticed how loosely he had tied us back together.

"I wasn't supposed to stay here this long, but I'll be back tonight I promise," he said as he got up vigorously and ran up the stairs.

A few hours went by, and Victoria had fallen deeply asleep. My eyelids felt very heavy too, but there was too much in my mind. Thoughts about everything scratched my brain and kept it from disconnecting. And what ached the most: where was Edric? Eventually, I tried to assure myself that everything would work out and that Victoria needed me here, and I needed to calm down. It was mid-day, and we could hear everyone above us working and moving things around, but no one came downstairs. Even if we were at about one hundred degrees, we were in what could be the darkest place in the entire boat. Surrendering, I cuddled as best as I could against my best friend and fell asleep too.

After what felt like a short 10-minute nap, I was awoken by a strong thud beside me. Thinking maybe it was just a dream, I tried going back to sleep when I felt Victoria jabbing my left elbow awakening me again. That's when I saw Jimmy all beaten and tied up, being thrown down the stairs as if he was one of the wooden barrels they would dispose of down here at times. The cruel men grunted and left right away, mocking him harshly and calling him a traitor and a soft hearted renegade before locking us up again. A soft tear glided down Jimmy's face as he tried to sit up. Victoria and I untied ourselves and untied him too. While I worked his feet free, Victoria pressed her palm against his cheek and cleaned off what seemed to be a mix of blood and dirt with a white tissue she carried in her back pocket.

Finally, I dared to ask, "What happened Jimmy?"

Although it was kind of obvious that they had boxed him up down here with us.

Jimmy opened his black eye as much as he could and looked at me for a split second explaining how everyone had found out that he had the intentions of helping us. Even though everyone on that ship was mad at him and his actions, they were his only family, and now they completely distrusted him. He was now a prisoner with us too. Victoria kissed his cheek carefully avoiding his wounds while we sat there in silence.

I felt terribly guilty for putting the only person who had tried to help us in this situation in harms way, and I know Victoria felt the same. I couldn't help but wonder who was behind all this. Who could possibly wish something this bad on us? That's when it hit me. Dreadful Mr. Gordon. I jumped up as fury made my veins curl inside me. That insane man probably wanted us dead, but why was he making us go through all this nonsense? And how did he know about this place and the pirates? Well, after all I've been through these past few days, anything could be possible, right?

I told Victoria about Mr. Gordon and even though we both agreed this was a bit too extreme for him to do, it was the only logical explanation we could find.

14

"Someone's coming!" The three of us tied ourselves up again as we heard the footsteps and the lock unlocking from the outside.

We sat close together in a circle back to back, waiting; no one really opened that door for just anything, and no one checked on us, so if someone was coming then it meant something was going on. I couldn't stop grinding my teeth, and my palms were slippery, flooded in cold sweat. I figured Victoria was as scared as I was, so I attempted to grab a hold of her hand when I noticed Jimmy had already taken care of that. It didn't surprise me at all, judging by how he glimpsed at her every time he had a chance; how his eyes would connect to hers every single time they made eye contact. I smiled for a moment, lost in my thoughts when the trap door finally banged open, and my eyes popped back into reality.

A big belly covered in a brownish apron with patterns of darker greasy smudges stomped down the stairs with its two little legs, holding a metal pot and three wooden bowls on top of it covering the face but reflecting the sunlight from above that shone on the bald spot crowning the figure. I sat up straight as I felt the sweat running out through my hair and tickling my temple, to then reach my chin. I could tell Victoria and Jimmy were just as altered. The man uncovered his face and left the utensils right next to me on the floor. He then uncovered the hefty metal stove and pouring, more like dropping, what seemed like watery oatmeal in every bowl without attempting to bend over, splattered slimy oats all over me. I tried as hard as I could to not say anything to him. Suddenly my fear turned to annoyance as I felt more heavy drops of food on my skin. As the man turned around to go back up, I opened my mouth and filled my lungs, about to say a few things to him when another cold hand that wasn't mine covered my lips and kept me from signing my own murder note.

The frustrated cook locked us back in the room again without looking back, when the hand jerked away from my mouth. I looked at Victoria and then at Jimmy with angered eyebrows, but both of them shrunk their shoulders telling me none of them had done anything. I started looking around when finally I looked above me. There he was, floating like when we had floated above the clouds.

"Edric, it's you!"

I untied myself and jumped up tangling my arms around his neck like a pretzel and pulled him back down to the floor. Edric smiled and hugged me tight right back. It took a while for me to let go, then he turned around and recharged his white smile as he hugged Victoria filled with enthusiasm.

"G' day, you must be Edric," Jimmy smiled in acceptance as Edric nodded and returned his handshake. "I've heard tons bout you bloke."

Edric smiled mischievously and shot a glance at me as we noticed Victoria melting with his accent. You might think she'd already gotten used to it, but not her; Edric and I had known her down to the bone for quite a while and how much different manners of speaking fascinated her every time.

"How did you get in here? How did you get in here without them seeing you? And how on earth did you learn to levitate like that? Or was that just me seeing things? I think this boat is driving me literally crazy little by little." Victoria almost jumped up and down with excitement while asking him tons of questions.

"Well," he began. "I wasn't levitating."

"The bullet tree! Remember? Becs told us all about it that night when I brought down the flake n' squid cut lunch," interrupted Jimmy just as excited, placing his hand on Victoria's shoulder.

"Right. But only I get to call her Becs, get that clear fella."

Said Edric, with the driest tone I had heard in a while.

I felt perplexed at his comment, yet a faint smile slipped around as I looked down at my feet. Victoria called me that sometimes too, but surely Edric didn't mean to be rude I guess.

"You see Vics; there's a broken window in the far back of the basement of this boat, and luckily I flew right in and stumbled upon you guys and not the lads up there with the eye patches. I was lucky to get Becs out of trouble as usual before she said anything to that baboon."

We chuckled and hugged each other; even Jimmy, who was now a part of us too.

I couldn't erase my smile; I was so happy to see him, to see us all together finally once again. But then I noticed that yeah, we were all together again, but deep inside the claws of a mad pirate ship. The baby hairs beside my ears stiffened as I frowned and punched Edric's right arm as usual.

"You moron, now you are stuck in here too! How are we even getting out of here? Now you are a prisoner too," I admonished.

"Look, at least, we are all together again. All we need is a plan. I overheard some men saying something about a captain who gave orders to catch you two for some kind of trap. And they mentioned me too; they know everything about me, even what happened to me and why everything about me changed that night when I turned 17. I'm surprised you two stayed by my side when all that happened. Especially you, Becky. You took care of me that stormy night when I broke into your house looking like I was insane. That's one of the many little things and actions you display that make such a firm base of how much Vics and I appreciate you," Edric said.

Anyway, they know everything, and there's a reason why it's us here. Jimmy you've got no idea who this captain is?" Edric continued.

Jimmy shook his head disappointed while scratching the back of his neck. But suddenly a light bulb seemed to appear inside his eyeballs as if lighting up his thoughts.

"I sure have not become personally acquainted with the cap. He's new on board which makes it a tad rare for him to be the captain already. But ya see lad; we sailors do anything for money. He must've blackmailed most of the crew to follow his orders and make him the new captain of this rotting ship. I have not heard of his name, but I can tell yous that he's from a small city, that one you mentioned last night actual-ay, where yous go ta school and ride colorful mopeds."

Open mouthed, Edric, Victoria and I looked at each other. It had to be Mr. Gordon; that was it! He used part of the money from the robbery at the jewelry store to bribe the pirates and make us go through all of this. But there was still something odd about it. Some pieces of the puzzle were still missing, but I couldn't figure them out just yet.

"He's not getting away with this," said Victoria. "We have to do something! But where even are we?"

"Vics we are in the middle of the Bermuda Triangle. That's where this island is located and why every boat or plane that crosses the triangle gets lost at sea. The island's deep powers trap anyone who attempts to get here."

I couldn't believe Edric's words. It all seemed so unreal to me, and yet at the end, I believed every word he said.

"Ok Ed, let's pretend everything you just said is true. How do you explain Mr. Gordon being a part of this? How did he get here? And how did you fly all the way here?"

I stood in front of him, defying him. I wanted answers. He signaled us to calm down with his hands and took a hold of his head with embarrassment in his eyes. We all sat down, and he began.

"Ok guys, here's something I wasn't planning on telling you because it's just not something worth talking about anyway."

Victoria and I glanced at each other astonished. Edric never hid anything from us; at least, that's what we thought.

"You both know I don't like talking about my father. Remember how Chuck's dad and mine had an accident right before coming back home from one of their expeditions? How they both passed away right before coming home?"

We both nodded and gestured him to keep narrating his story.

"Well, my dad was a great father, he knew how interesting all these things were for me, and he also knew about all these powers and changes I would get when I turned 17. Anyway, he and chuck's dad, Mr. Morris, had figured out a way to explore the Bermuda Triangle using a mechanism no one had figured out," Edric continued.

"We all know the story of the Bermuda Triangle, but they found a way in to explore it. My dad would send me letters in every one of his expeditions and this time he sent me one of the maps to this island and everything they had found out about it little by little. I was so excited and eager to know more. I wished for him to get back so that he would take me to this mystery island himself and I could see all these wonders he talked about in his letters! The thing is guys, discoveries like these are worth millions of dollars and my father wanted it all to himself, or so I was told by my mother who read it in the letter that Mrs. Morris received from her husband right before he passed away. That's why I hate talking about what happened. It's hard for me to face the fact that my father would be so selfish and corrupt as not to give Mr. Morris any credit at all.

His face slowly washed out and gloomed, as he disconnected his eyes from ours.

"I mean, we've been part of their family for years. And Chuck; it's hard for me to look at him without feeling terrible about it. So, my father attempted to steal everything; all their findings from Mr. Morris for money to later get trapped in his own trap. I guess that's how Mr. Gordon got ahold of the location of the island and almost or all the information about it; he was involved in the situation and probably found the map in the evidence room or something."

We all sat quietly, evaluating the situation in our heads and how it all made sense now not knowing what to say.

Edric tried to hide the anguish he was feeling and looked down at his knees while he rubbed his hands together nervously. I could tell he was embarrassed too, and I couldn't believe such a cool guy like his father would do something like that; he had always been Edric's hero. All this was so much to handle. Everything that had been going on with his father after his death, Victoria getting trapped, then me, and just everything in general.

I sat closer to Edric and placed my arm around his back trying to comfort him right before he let out some deep sobs I had never heard before. He untangled himself and hugged me back as I enfolded him with both my arms like I had done several times in the past. Except this time it was different; he was like a small hopeless child. Victoria and Jimmy looked at us, still in shock as Victoria moved closer on the other side of him and she too cuddled him in her arms on top of mine. It was something sad to watch I guess.

We had finally cracked the code but in return, we had also cracked our best friend. I could imagine this was something he never talked about with anyone, even if we all knew how much he missed his father.

15

Being trapped in that wooden oven of a boat was bad, but being trapped inside that boat while there was a thunderstorm going on outside was even worse. It was as if the waves were working hard on agitating the boat so much it would tip over! We rolled from side to side, falling on top of each other. I felt as if I was inside a snow globe in the hands of a small child. There was a point when I thought the possibility of giants living on the island was not slight at all, but then I realized that it was in fact just a cruel act of the ocean itself when cold water began running in through the same broken window Edric had come in through.

The water was rising, the storm was getting louder, desperation was overflowing, but we all knew this would be the perfect opportunity to escape. It seemed unreal, how much the boat rocked from side to side, back and forth, up and down. I lost my balance completely and hit my head against the little stairs leading to the exit, but I tried to get up quickly and felt the sting of salt water as bloody goo slid and covered my eyebrow. The four of us got separated with rough movements of the boat, but Edric took ahold of us rapidly and calmed our nerves a little by holding Victoria and me by the wrists; while Jimmy held Victoria's on the other side.

The water was already covering my foot. It had very suddenly reached my ankle, and I hadn't even noticed how fast it rose. Edric looked around in a determined need to get us out of there and pulled us closer together.

"Ok guys, we have to try and break the door open with the movement of the boat, rock back and forth with it and try as hard as you can to push that door open using your own bodies," Edric said over the sound of the storm.

"But Edric," said Victoria, almost screaming. "What if we get out, and those monsters catch us again?"

Edric explained in a rush how with this storm going on they would have other things to worry about, and we weren't more valuable to them than their own lives which was why this was the perfect moment to escape. We would get out and run all the way to the other side of the boat where he had seen the captain's room which would probably have bullet seeds hidden somewhere for a quick escapade.

Edric stumbled and almost fell as he kept talking, but seemed to keep calm in a failed attempt to keep our nerves less stressed. The weather seemed to be getting tougher and tougher as we ran one way to the other, hitting the trap door as hard as we could with our body weight; but to me, it seemed useless.

The boat, as if knowing we were trying to escape, hit a wave so hard that it knocked all of us at once. I blacked out for just a second when Edric tugged on my shoulder and helped me up holding my hand and keeping both of us balanced. I saw the look in his eyes and how scared he seemed as a small drop of water molded itself around his left eye. That's when I looked down and saw the water already towering my knees.

"We have to hurry up and get out of here!" I screamed in

desperation, still a bit dizzy. I couldn't really see anyone else but Edric next to me.

He helped me get stable, and we spotted Victoria and Jimmy on the other side struggling to get up as well. This was harder than I thought, and hope was even harder to keep.

I can't recall ever drinking so much salt water. I felt it inside my nose. I felt it scratching my throat on the inside. I could feel it flooding my lungs, and I could also feel it already reaching my armpits.

We went back and forth with the boat. We tried as hard as we could, and when that didn't work, we tried harder. Adrenaline rushed back and forth within us, and I could feel and see blood around me that wasn't necessarily mine. I started sobbing. I felt as if I was inside a horrible night terror and I knew right then right there that these were probably the last minutes we would be together.

Victoria stopped pushing as well and hugged me as she spotted the bruises all over her white arms and her tears mixed in with the salt water already reaching her chin. Edric and Jimmy grunted, grinding their teeth and putting all their weight on that door as if their lives depended on it, which in fact was actually what was going on. But Victoria and I felt hopeless. Soon, we had to keep our chins upward to be able to breathe, which was the moment when I figured that even if swimming out through the broken window was a death sentence for sure, it was better than just drowning in here without trying.

I managed to pull Jimmy and Edric away from the trapdoor for a second to try and convince them to swim to the back and get out from there. Thankfully, they didn't put too much of a fight and moved when I called them over; because right that same second a wooden mast struck by thick lightning collapsed to the floor and destroyed the little trap door we had been trying to open. Edric grabbed my face with both hands and kissed my cheek hard. If I hadn't made them move, then he and Jimmy would've cracked their skulls open with the collapsing of the pole. For a second, I forgot how scared I was and gave thanks for being alive.

We swam upwards to the deck and tried to keep our balance as we took the next step.

"I don't know about you guys, but I think that having swum through the broken window downstairs would've been safer than getting up here, even considering the vast amount of dangerous sea creatures around," said Victoria

I could barely hear what she was screaming over the storm haunting the boat. Ugly sea marauders of all types and sizes ran back and forth from starboard to port, tripping on their own rags and breathing more water than air; we too were soaking wet. It felt as if we were already sunken along with the ship.

"Look for the captain's cabin!"

"There!" I pointed almost as soon as Edric finished his sentence.

A wooden-rimmed door with glass windows shattered all over the place sat on the very top back part of the deck. Despite the disaster going on, it still looked fancy and warm on the inside with a welcoming glow of kerosene lamps lighting it up. Inside the cabin, more broken glass pieces, objects flying around and a shadow sitting down on its captain chair with no worries at all, a very, extremely familiar shadow I was sure I had seen before.

We ran, slipping but not falling all the way back, dodging the crazy men who had lost their minds, not even thinking of a plan just running in hopes of finding the bullet seeds to get out of that mad house. I felt the water drops as they whipped my face. I couldn't see very well, but I ran with all the strength I had left, squinting my eyes following the faint glow looking right at that so familiar shadow, scared to death.

I was so concentrated on getting there that I hadn't noticed the storm was passing and even though the boat had practically been sinking, it was still afloat. Another crucial thing that slipped away was how all of a sudden I was running all by myself. I looked back in one sudden movement and saw Edric, Victoria, and Jimmy, all tied up, each of them being held by a different man. I stood there surrounded; my tears raced down my cheeks once again. We weren't just ordinary prisoners; I knew something else was going on. How could we be that important as not to let us escape? I knew Mr. Gordon had something to do with all this; he had to be that demented captain.

Before I stopped running, Jimmy fiddled his head and bit the hand of the fat buccaneer who held his mouth shut right where he seemed to have lost a finger and screamed,

"Rebecca, keep running!"

I saw my friends being held captive. Crying and angry I finally understood why Edric had trapped himself in that horrid place just to try and save us. I got so angry my blood boiled as I thought about everything that was going on; and as I felt one filthy hand barely touching my shoulder, I turned around and spotted a crooked nose fast enough to break it with my elbow and keep running. I ran far enough to almost reach the door of the captain, but even I knew twenty men would eventually be able to get a hold of one girl.

While I was being tied up and taken back with my friends, I fought and kicked and screamed, managing to break a little brittle glass window as I kicked in the direction of the so very familiar shadow. Everyone stayed put as we all noticed the shadow getting up from its chair as it seemed to put a small teacup down. The pirates let us go as their jaws dropped petrified, and small drops of water flew in their mouths like flies. I sprinted towards my friends and untied them. Victoria hugged me and grunted in anguish over my shoulder right before we turned around, frightened by the mysterious shadow that wasn't that mysterious after all.

The four of us walked slowly towards the shadow as the pirates walked backward and stared with their faces solidified in shock more afraid than us. I walked in front of my friends in a scared but more curious manner. The shadow approached the door, and no one said a word. We heard the crack of the door as it opened, and waited patiently with nerve-wracking feelings exploding inside.

The shadow soon became a figure and stepped outside into the rain with us. Victoria gasped and covered her mouth in amusement. Edric popped his eyes open and took a couple of steps forward as he noticed I almost lost my balance at the sight. But he didn't unglue his eyes to those eyes we had seen multiple times before.

Jimmy, who stood behind the three of us, tugged cautiously on my sleeve and murmured a soft question, "So, that's Mr. Gordon?"

I couldn't believe what I was seeing. Light, familiar eyes which now just looked dark green in plain evil, and red curls storming out of that black leatherette pirate hat as if he hadn't cut his hair in ages. Millions of freckles were on the face of a so-called captain that had held us captive. The same one that had kidnaped Victoria some nights ago and the same one who had been sitting in my living room uncountable times. The hair, the freckles, the face, the eyes.

"No," I replied, catching my breath before I could finish. "That's Chuck."

16

"Chuckster, is that really you?" Edric took a few steps forward. It had taken a while before he managed to mumble those few words. His eyes sure weren't enough proof of what was right in front of him.

"What's up with the new look chicken legs?"

Chuck came closer to Edric and grunted. I had never noticed how deep his voice could be.

"Why are you doing this?"

Edric seemed so confused; so disappointed, he couldn't seem to understand. But as upset as he was, his fury and impatience for answers was much stronger.

"Edric; fragile little rat, don't you understand? The reason you are here is your own father's fault. Ever since he died along with my dear father, I have wanted to seek nothing more than vengeance for his memory, and what better revenge than his own blood."

Edric seemed just as confused and hurt.

"But Chuck, it was all one big accident! Don't you remember?

Don't you remember we said we would be brothers forever despite what had happened?"

What had happened? None of us had heard the actual story. My dad had never talked about it, and Edric had always told us he didn't know anything either. But apparently he did. I looked at Victoria as we stood behind Edric and I knew she was thinking the same thing. What was Edric hiding from us?

"You don't know do you, Rebecca, he never told you." Chuck locked his eyes on mine, curving a sketchy smile with his thick lips.

"Little Victoria doesn't know either does she? Edric, I thought you and Rebecca didn't hide anything from each other. Isn't that what you've always confided me; that you are that close? Why don't you tell her the truth Edric? Tell her now."

Chuck came down those three little steps that separated us, more intimidating than ever, but that was the last thing I could think about in that instant.

"Tell us what, Edric," said Victoria, her face red just like her mother's tomato paste.

Edric looked down to the wet wooden beams, twirling his fingers as he searched for the right words.

"What is it Edric?"

I knew the last thing he needed was more people against him, so I put my hand on his shoulder and tried to comfort him just a tiny bit.

Edric kept mumbling; he couldn't seem to put all his thoughts into words.

"What is it Edric? Come on tell us what's going on!" Victoria was losing her patience, and in my head, I was too.

Edric finally looked up again as he frowned in anger and embarrassment. Chuck eyed Edric and grabbed him by the neck turning him around to face us.

"If it weren't because of your little friend's father, mine would not be dead."

I didn't know what he was talking about, and neither did Victoria or Jimmy, but we looked at Edric for an explanation or something that could make what Chuck had just said something untrue; unfortunately that was not to be.

"When we were told that our parents had had an accident, Chuck and I also received some of the stuff that belonged to them including a video diary Chuck's dad had been filming throughout their voyages. Chuck and I kept it secret from everyone else and watched it by ourselves. At first, it was kind of boring and monotone, but then it started getting interesting. First, it was just new discoveries and misunderstandings, then bigger fights between both our fathers, then plain avarice. They soon became enemies, and we could hear all their conversations. One day, the day we decided it was best to stop watching the video diaries, that was the worse day I can remember."

Edric paused for a moment and looked straight at me as if trying to apologize with his eyes; as if whatever he was about to tell me would affect our friendship in some way. I gave him a comforting half smile to let him know everything was fine; he got the memo and went on with his story.

"There had been some kind of gas leak inside the submarine, so both of them were wearing face masks; they both knew they'd most likely die that day. So Mr. Morris held his camera around showing all the maps and information they had gathered before it was all gone. Then there's the worse part. When Chuck's father had found the nearest exit, you see my father hiding under some tubes waiting for him. When Mr. Morris climbs up the stairs holding the 360 waterproof camera with its precious information in it, he held his free hand down for his friend to get a hold of it and help him get out. You can clearly see my dad hitting him in the head with a pipe, grabbing the camera with greed, and climbing up the stairs himself. To make it worse, when he's climbing outside, the submarine hits something and makes him stumble unconsciously falling to the ground. The camera records everything including how after a couple of minutes the submarine starts sinking fast and both of them drown."

I didn't know what to do next. I could see Edric's eyes filled with guilt for something that ate him on the inside while Chuck smiled comfortably, as he noticed how shocking the news was to us.

"So, this is why you kidnapped us? Vengeance for something we didn't have anything to do with? Something that isn't even Edric's fault?" I said.

A bitter taste filled my mouth as I digested everything, but I still couldn't bear to believe how someone as close to us as Chuck could be that resentful against his best friend.

Chuck came closer to me, finally giving Edric some space to breath; this was harder for him than for any of us. His freckled nose almost touched mine, almost as if we were competing to see whose face was glowering the most.

"See, Becs," he said in a tremendously sardonic voice that made me boil on the inside even more. "Edric, as you might have noticed, has gone through certain changes giving him a much stronger aptitude; something almost impossible in my criteria. He's doing things such as flying without the necessity of anything but himself."

A meaningful perplexed look showed on my face. Edric couldn't fly. We used the bullet seeds; that's how he flies. I thought to myself, Chuck is just trying to confuse us even more.

"Oh, I guess he hasn't told you that either. Your friend Edric here, he has some special abilities. I thought he had, at least, told you that! It seems like this is a pot of lies he has been keeping from you huh, Edric? Anyway, taking Edric would've been something almost impossible for these fools to do by themselves so I thought it would be better for him to come to us. See, Victoria was an easy catch, and then you! That was a mine of gold for us; he would come get you for sure. And just as planned, he did."

"Fine, but now what? You'll feed us to the sharks? Don't you think that's a bit extreme?" After asking, I knew I shouldn't have. He had such a wolfish expression that for the first time after seeing him, I felt truly scared.

"You read me, like an open book Rebecca."

He took his eyes of off mine and signaled his men to take a hold of us again but gripped my wrist tight before I could move. His fixed expression hurt me on the inside, but I wasn't going to let him know that.

Edric's pained look turned into a dark one as he let himself go savagely and threw a punch at Chuck, pummeling his left eye and pitching him to the floor. Right then, the storm struck the boat once again, and lightning flashed. Some helped Chuck up while others went for Jimmy and Victoria who put up a fight for us so we could proceed with the plan even though it would be useless after a few seconds. Edric then took a hold of my hand, and we darted to Chuck's glass cabin almost falling because of how fast Edric was going. I couldn't help but think of what Chuck had said and all the things Edric had been hiding from us.

We locked the door and searched frantically for the seeds to get out of there. My hair was flying everywhere and even if we dismantled the place, we couldn't find anything. We heard shots outside. My heart stopped for a second thinking that could have gone through one of our friends, but then I noticed how the bullets were, in fact, piercing the few glass windows left around us.

"Edric, we have to get out of here! We won't find anything! There are no seeds!"

Edric kept flipping the furniture around and throwing small pieces of burnt candles and wooden figurines over his head. He seemed so absent and focused on finding our only escape; he had always been such a hot head. I rolled my eyes and tried to talk him out of it, but he wouldn't listen. More bullets were fired when I felt one of them as it grazed my shoulder. I took a handful of Edric's arm and dragged him outside with strength I didn't know I had determined to get us both out of that trap. The wind was blowing so hard; I felt how it pushed me, trying to throw me into the water with all the sea creatures and terrible monsters. I didn't know what to do next. The men kept shooting and Edric and I just rolled down trying to disappear. I couldn't imagine a way out now. The men formed a stampede towards us, and I covered my eyes like a little girl. It all happened so fast.

When the impossible happened.

For the first time, the storm seemed to be on our side as it hit and almost flipped the boat. Edric held me tight and levitated off of the ground while all the men slid down the deck and into the furious waters. I cracked open my fingers and watched the scene, noticing how Edric, in fact, could fly without any seeds.

The boat seized, but the storm didn't. We felt so disoriented and frantic feelings mixed with adrenaline flowed between us. Edric looked for Victoria and Jimmy with a brooding appearance, just as worried as I was. Lightning struck once again bringing a frosty wind with it. That's when I figured that by now the boat should have sunk already. Why was it still afloat? I ran to the edge of the boat and looked around for an explanation, forgetting how psychotic it was around me and forgetting how strong the storm was. A wave hit the boat and threw me overboard leaving me almost dangling. Fortunately, Edric had noticed and helped me up again. That's when we perceived, on the side of the boat a little further away, a woman, eyes closed, and her hands expanded outward saying something we couldn't hear. Parallel to her, another woman was doing the same thing.

They seemed to be really glazed and concentrated, judging by everything that was going on.

"Who are they?" I asked.

Edric stared at them mischievously and said, "Becs those are witches, they seem to be keeping the boat from sinking! I've got a plan, but first, we have to find Jimmy and Victoria."

We ran back to the main area of the deck, ignoring the fallen pirates and the wooden parts of the boat ripping apart around us. I looked up to where the pirate flag used to be held and finally saw both of them tied with the same thick rope we had seen all along. I was so tired of that bloody rope!

"Why are they up there?" I asked even though I could imagine the answer.

"Chuck probably tied them up there as a lightning rod; we have to get them down now!"

"Edric," I said. "If it's true that you can fly, just go up there and get our friends. I don't know why you didn't tell us about this, but I'm not mad, just please get them before something happens!"

"That was exactly my plan, Becs." He jumped up, except it wasn't a jump because he didn't come back down.

I lost sight of him with a curtain of rain and waited for him cautiously guarding my back against any decrepit body that came near me. I looked back up and squinted my eyes covering them a little with my hands to try and see what was going on up there, trying not to slip again. Edric wasn't just able to fly; he was so much stronger. I saw him rip that rope with his bare hands and take Jimmy and Victoria in his arms then bring them down to me. Now the four of us were together again. Edric panted in a quick breathing that unmasked how shamefaced, and how exhausted he was.

"Guys, I know I've hidden things from you, but I was just scared and mostly embarrassed, please forgive me."

Victoria and I hugged him and smiled at him. "This doesn't mean you got away without explaining! But first, let's get out of here," Victoria said as her confidence was reinforced.

"Reckon! What's the plan, Capt'n?" Jimmy jolted up excitedly, completely ignoring the blizzard.

17

We separated and followed the plan. Jimmy and Victoria had gone to one end, and I would go to the other leaving Edric to look for what he had to look for. I could barely see through the storm, and it only got stronger. Time ran out, and the witches would probably flee soon.

I got to the tip of the ship and found nothing, so I ran dead ahead above deck back against the wind feeling the water drops whipping my face once again. But that wouldn't take me down again. I had noticed that all of us were stronger than we thought. I found Jimmy and Victoria up the stairs opening and closing doors that seemed like small closets where we found two wooden brooms. Jimmy grasped both of them, and we followed him downstairs looking for Edric. The witches instantly opened their eyes when they felt how their only true possession was being removed from its hiding place. The ship began to sink, faster than I thought, as the witches chased after us and followed our scent, dismissing their obligation to keep the ship afloat.

Where was Edric?

The three of us rushed looking for Edric and separated in hopes of finding him making it harder for the witches to find us. I decided to start by the same place where I had almost fallen into the water before. The situation got scarier each second. The witches had stopped keeping the boat from sinking so once again the water was winning over the ship furiously.

I turned around and felt something pulling me up and upside down by the ankle; it was one of them. She had somehow become uglier and more intimidating than how she looked before. Her eyes were a deep black, thriving a dark look as she scanned me from toe to head; she lifted me up and sniffed my cheek as if that would help her figure out something. I felt one of her warts brush my face. It was repugnant; her pale fingers felt my ears and she scratched my neck desperately as if any of those things would get her broom back. That's when I couldn't help myself any longer. I burst and yelled for Edric to come help me, but she flicked her dilapidated finger and covered my mouth in a slimy material throwing me back to the floor. I sat up with a sore body and felt a hard ache in the back of my head. One fat tear ran down my face when I saw her horrid expression of disgust towards me; and she pointed one long, rickety nail in my direction. I looked away with downcast eyes expecting the worse when all of a sudden Edric jumped in front of me and held a metal box towards the witch making her spell bounce back to herself. She screeched and recoiled while her skin burned to dust.

We stared slack-jawed, but Edric got me up and ripped that thing away from my lips, hugging me tight and then taking me to look for Jimmy and Victoria. There was water everywhere, and it was hard to walk, the water was freezing cold, and we could barely move. Then, we saw the two brooms floating our way; Edric swam quick and got a hold of them which was when we spotted Jimmy and Victoria running our way and being chased by the other witch, who cast her spells towards them from behind and luckily missed every time. Edric threw one broom to Jimmy, Victoria and I each sat behind one of them hoping the plan would work, hoping that Edric was right about these brooms. The witch was coming closer and closer. I closed my eyes and held on tight to Edric when the two brooms flew up in the air avoiding masts and falling wooden panels. We flew out of there, and the whole thing sank into the arms of the ocean.

18

The four of us got to the shore and laughed in relief. We had gotten out of there alive, and it was still hard to process all that had happened. Throwing ourselves on the sand in exhaustion, we contemplated the sun waking up, warming our skin and turning the water a calming turquoise while the salty air brushed our faces. Edric was still carrying that tin box with him, but I decided it was better to ask more about it later; there were many things to talk about and right now was not the right time to do so.

"I think it's finally time to go home," Edric said as we all looked at him and smiled in agreement.

"You can come with us too, Jimmy, if you want. We can say you are an exchange student or something; we will figure it out!" Victoria said sounding excited to take him home with us. But we all knew that wasn't something easy for him or anyone else.

"See Victoria, it was ripper to have met ya mates, but there are many things I gotta take care of here before leaving." He took her hand and looked at her to make it easier for her to understand; she nodded and smiled back not saying a word.

That same morning, we left for home after saying goodbye to Jimmy and promising it wouldn't be the last time we saw each other. We took off riding the stolen brooms.

"I'll send letters!" Jimmy waved from the shore brightening his face once again smiling as hard as he could.

The way back seemed so short, but after all I had seen, it wasn't hard to believe how much magic there could be hidden just anywhere.

19

My bed was still warm. It wasn't hard to guess that the three of us were grounded for a long, long time. Of course, no one would believe any part of our story if we ever told it, so it was best just to keep it to ourselves.

That same night, I put on a jacket and sneakers, slid out the window quietly and headed out to the abandoned house for an informational meeting Victoria, Edric and I had planned. There was half a moon in the sky with twinkly stars hiding behind the clouds but coming out sometimes to say hello; it was a plain, normal night. No one came after me, no monsters chased me, no one was following me. It was comforting to think that the worse that could happen would be my parents finding out I sneaked out which really wouldn't cause anything because they couldn't ground me more than I was already.

I got to the house, and Victoria was there already sitting on the small steps. She handed me some candy when I sat next to her, and she could only talk about when she would get Jimmy's first letter. We giggled and chatted like we hadn't in a while; it was nice. A loud thud scared me for a second and then I saw it was just Edric jumping inside with us. After all that had happened, I was still a bit paranoid. He shook his muddy boots and sat next to me. I handed him his favorite sour-green-apple candy, and we both looked at him like spectators waiting for his story.

"Ok, so your powers, what's that all about?" I asked after seeing he was having trouble thinking of how to begin.

Edric bit his sugary green strap and brushed his short hair back with his other hand as he began.

"As you both know, my grandfather and great-grandfather had been cartographers as well with the exception that like my father, they weren't just ordinary cartographers. All of them knew there are inexplicable things in this world that people don't dare to look into, like the island, so all of them dedicated their lives to finding these rare places. My father had known Mr. Morris for a long time and didn't mind letting him in all the family secrets. That's why they did all these great things together, I guess he then regretted it. Anyway, my great grandfather found a place he never told anyone about where he found a special treasure. It was not an ordinary one; it was something you can't grab with your bare hands. After he had found this, he got some, let's say, extraordinary abilities. When my father turned my age, he got them too, and now it was my turn. I guess it will keep happening to my children and grandchildren as well, who knows. This is what my father and Chuck's were looking for all these years; that's the treasure Chuck talked about, and our parents most likely found it right before the accident. That is what this little tin box will help us figure out I hope. This is the same box that was given to Chuck and me; the same one that contains the videos. I let Chuck keep it in his house because I didn't think it was a big deal at all, just old maps, papers, and the videos. I thought, of course, it belonged to both of us, and it never crossed my mind that any of this could happen."

I nodded. Of course, none of us thought this could be possible.

Now that I thought about it, where was Chuck?

"Guys, when we left the ship, we saw everyone drowning and running around, but where was Chuck? The last time I saw him, Edric punched him and then he just disappeared. Victoria, did you see him?"

She shook her head wide-eyed, "Well, maybe he just drowned? Or he left somehow. Maybe that's why there were no seeds."

"Becs and I would've seen him flying away or drowning. I mean we saw all the other men drowning and the witches. There's no way. Plus, it was Chuck we're talking about guys. He must've had a Plan B under his sleeve."

We talked about Chuck for hours; it just seemed eerie I guess. But after a while, we were just glad we were safe and together again. It began getting a bit chilly. The crickets sang in a well-organized manner as the wet puddles reflected the pale lights from the moon and stars. We sat close together with frosted noses and colorful candy bags.

"So Ed," I began. "Are we opening the box?"

Edric shook his head. "I don't want to open it Becs; I want to bury it, right here, in a safe place where no one will find it, but I will always know its exact location. Besides, all that's in here are old maps and passageways to poisonous information that is not worth looking for. This would only bring us more trouble if more people find out about it. I say we bury it and forget about it. What do you guys think?"

Victoria and I looked at each other as usual and agreed; so that was what we did. We dug out a hole and Edric threw in the box burying his own remorse with it.

20

Victoria and I wrapped the gift in a hurry. It looked wrinkled, and you could see little triangles of my mom's clear tape sticking out; not to mention we had used last year's Christmas paper, but we were so late!

We ran up and down the stairs always forgetting something, but this time, we were ready to leave. It was Edric's birthday, and we wanted to be the first ones to get there. Victoria finished applying final touches of eyeliner as I kissed my mother goodbye and we headed to the bakery shop for a big chocolate cake, his favorite! Victoria and I didn't even knock the door. We lit up 20 candles on the front porch and stepped into the house with no invitation.

"Good evening Mrs. Be… I mean Mrs. Garrett!" I said.

"Hello, Mrs. Garrett!" Victoria added.

"Hello, girls!" she replied, fixing her golden locks; happy to see us as usual.

We walked smiling in excitement right past her and her new husband Luke Garrett, whose last name she had decided to take even though Edric would keep his father's. Edric Becker, it was nicer than "Edric Garrett" according to me. But Edric's stepfather seemed like a nice man. He was always really friendly to everyone. Edric was sitting on the kitchen counter nibbling on one of his mother's chocolate chip cookies she had baked for the special occasion.

"Happy Birthday, old man!"

We put the birthday cake in front of him and watched the faint candle glow reflect on his white teeth. He blew out the candles and hugged us both. Edric seemed delighted and really cheerful. He wore a huge smile and a nice button down white shirt to accompany it. The truth is, we were all quite excited. It had been a good couple of weeks, and everything seemed to have fallen into place. I kissed his cheek hard leaving a trace of lipstick and watched his smile getting wider and his cheeks blushing while Victoria ran to the drawer and got a knife to cut what we called the pre-birthday-birthday cake.

Edric's mom walked in the room radiant eyes and smiley face followed by Mr. Garrett.

"Edric, before more people get here, there's something I need to give you. She stood next to Edric and brushed her fingers through his hair like she had done ever since he was a small boy.

"Your father, he was a very good man and even after all the things I've seen and heard, I don't believe for one second that he could kill a fly. To me, he will always be a brave, loving father to my son. Right before the accident, I received this letter which said it was for you on your 20th birthday."

Edric grabbed the letter out of her hands hastily interrupting her and sat down on the couch.

"After I saw it was for you, I did not read any further, Edric," she said in a loud, preoccupied voice towards him. Mr. Garrett put his hand on her shoulder and signaled her it was better to leave him alone for a bit.

Edric did not let anyone read the letter, but as soon as he finished he put on his jacket placing the thin piece of paper inside and pulled Victoria and me outside without saying a word. We got in his car, and he took off leaving a cloud of dust behind. He looked sullen and concentrated with a vacant look, inside his own thoughts.

"Ed, what's going on?" I asked.

"We have to get the tin box," he replied.

"What tin box?"

Victoria and I had no idea what was going on. It was puzzling, but we would find out soon. We got to the abandoned house, and Edric jumped inside so fast we couldn't keep up. He had gotten really athletic ever since he turned 17, exactly three years ago. He stood on the wet grass as if analyzing the area and then went back to his car taking a shovel out of the trunk and throwing it over the fence. Victoria and I just stood there waiting as he dug out the tin box that used to belong to his and Chuck's fathers. He climbed back out in a second and jolted back to the car, impatiently waiting for Victoria and me.

"I thought we had left this behind Ed. Why are we bringing it back?" Victoria talked to him as if she was scolding him for taking the box back, so I interrupted her brief interrogation and went on.

"So uh, what's the plan, Chief?"

He grinned at me in the reflection of the rear mirror and stepped harder on the gas. Victoria and I exchanged glances.

"Ed you are scaring us," I said

"We have to watch the tape again; the last one Chuck and I watched. The camera belonged to my father, not Chuck's. He was going to let me have it today."

We got back to the house and ran up the stairs as we headed to Edric's room and then opened the metal box with a screwdriver. He blew out the dust inside the box and threw out pieces of folded paper; maps and tiny clues. Finally finding the cassette labeled, "#31" and putting it inside a little black box that was connected to his laptop.

I put my hand on his right arm before he clicked the play button. "Edric, are you sure you want to watch this?"

He nodded unsure of himself and pressed play fast forwarding it to when Chuck's father was going up the stairs with the camera holding a hand down to Edric's father so they could both get out. We watched the scene a couple of times until Edric replayed it once again and paused it right when Chuck's father was climbing his last step before he was hit in the head. Edric looked closely at the picture and zoomed it in to where Chuck's father's hand was stretching downward. Mr. Morris' bare skin is shown for just one second under a red alarm light and as he stretches out his arm and uncovers the sleeve a little, we can kind of see his wrist where there's a specific birthmark in the shape of a leaf. Edric zooms in more, wide-eyed in a quizzical manner.

"My father did not kill Chuck's father...it was the other way around."

Edric sat staring at the picture as he uncovered his wrist. It was the same birthmark he had gotten himself the day he got his powers. The same leaf-shaped mark, exactly on the same spot.